A
Harlequin
Romance

LOVE HATH AN ISLAND

First published in 1970 by Mills & Boon Limited,
17 - 19 Foley Street, London, England.

Harlequin Canadian edition published September, 1971
Harlequin U.S. edition published December, 1971

Standard Book Number: 373-51522-7.

Printed in Canada

Love hath an island,
And I would be there;
Love hath an island,
And nurtureth there
For men the Delights
The beguilers of care,
Cyprus, Love's island;
And I would be there.

Over the hillsides,
And I would be there –
Olympian hillsides,
For Heaven is there
With spirits divine
And shining of fire;
And there are the Graces,
And there is Desire.

Euripides: The Bacchæ

CHAPTER ONE

As usual the café was packed. Mary stood gazing around, then began making her way between the tables to the far end where Josie was sitting, one hand raised and the other firmly placed on her handbag which occupied the chair by her side.

'So sorry I'm late.' Mary took off her coat and laid it over the back of the chair.

'Thought I'd never be able to save it.' Josie removed her bag and Mary sat down. 'The looks I've had – it's a wonder I'm alive!'

'Sorry,' Mary said again. 'Mr. Cartwright gave me a letter at the last minute.'

'He would! I can't think why you stay with that old slave-driver.'

'He isn't,' protested Mary, though not very convincingly. 'I hope I haven't made him sound an ogre. I strongly disapprove of disloyalty to one's employer.' She reached for the menu and they studied it together, deciding on steak and chips.

While they were waiting to be served Mary sat back, resigning herself to her friend's chatter, but after a short time her mind began to wander.

A strange friendship, she mused, watching the waitress as she took the order from the old lady at the next table. Josie, only nineteen, flighty, frivolous and extravagant, training to be a model merely as a relief from boredom – for she had no need to work at all. Mary, six years older, and just the opposite; practical and serious and 'too efficient and methodical to appeal to any man' Josie had once said teasingly, adding,

'Your life must be so dull, Mary; why don't you snap out of it! – do something impulsive for a change? It's fun. You'll never find a husband living the life you lead – office all day and that drab old flat at night; your books and records and a fortnight each year at the seaside. I'd go raving mad!'

The waitress came and they ordered; Josie continued to prattle on, hardly pausing for breath as she described some of the things she was learning at the school.

'And you must hold your hands with these two fingers together, it's more elegant. . . .'

Mary's eyes suddenly focused on the young couple a few tables away. Having noticed her, the man was now speaking to his companion. Then they both looked in Mary's direction. She lowered her eyes, but not in time to escape their glances of contempt.

Josie reached for the water jug, filled their glasses and then continued her inane and high-pitched chatter. Yes, a very odd friendship, but one for which Mary was grateful. For Josie, living miles away in the country, and travelling into the small town each day, was in total ignorance of Mary's 'past'.

They had met one day when, nearing her table, Josie had dropped her handbag and it had flown open. Mary helped her to pick up her belongings. The following day there happened to be an empty place at Mary's table and Josie had promptly occupied it and began talking to Mary as though she had known her all her life. From then on it became a regular thing for them to take their lunch together; the friendship had developed and a month ago Mary had spent a most restful and pleasant week-end at The Wardens, the delightful country house in Cheshire where the views from the terrace included the lovely foothills of the Welsh mountains.

Josie's mother, slight of build and beautifully groomed, was also of a serious disposition, very different from her daughter who, she said, took after her father.

'Adrian takes after me,' she smiled. 'And according to Josie he's dull.'

'Dull and pompous,' Josie put in. 'I'm glad he doesn't live at home.'

8

'You'd find your activities curtailed if he did.'

'That's why I'm glad he doesn't live at home!'

It had been so wonderful to get away for that week-end, away from the pointing fingers, the glances of contempt, wonderful to be with people who had no knowledge of the affair and, therefore, accepted her at her face value.

They were half-way through the meal when Josie exclaimed,

'Heavens, I almost forgot again! Mum told me to ask you yesterday. Will you come for the week-end?'

'This week-end? – but it's Friday, I couldn't be ready—'

'How stodgy you are; don't make excuses. You can do all those silly chores another time. Who cares if the crumbs on the floor stay till Monday?'

'There are no crumbs on my floor,' Mary retorted with faint indignation.

'I'll bet there aren't, knowing you – and no mice to clear them up if there were.' Josie laughed and Mary found herself laughing too. No doubt about it, Josie was good for her despite the difference in personalities. In fact Mary sometimes half wished she could be like her, if only for a little while, and, as Josie suggested, do something impulsive for a change. But Mary was too cautious, too practical.

Nevertheless, she had been a little like Josie once; not so scatterbrained, but vivacious and happy, popular with all her gay young crowd. She'd been invited to every party, always sought after and when, at twenty-one, she had become engaged to the famous footballer who was himself so popular and gay, Mary found herself more in demand than ever.

'You will come, you'll have to,' Josie was saying anxiously. 'Mum will be so mad if she knows I forgot yesterday. Besides, I told her – when she asked me last night – that you'd accepted. You can't let me down. And it will be good for Mum, she's feeling rather depressed.'

'Anything wrong?'

'It's Adrian. I told you a couple of months ago that he'd asked Mum to advertise for a secretary, didn't I?'

'A man secretary, you said,' returned Mary, nodding. 'Did your mother find someone suitable?'

'Only two men have applied – and she's kept advertising all this time. Men don't seem to jump at going out to these glamorous places like girls. Neither of these was suitable and Mum's beginning to despair of ever getting Adrian fixed up.' Josie's forehead puckered. 'Why do you suppose he wants a male secretary?'

'Can't think. Perhaps, as he has these plantations, these orange groves, he wants someone who can turn a hand to a little manual work in between.'

'Oh, no, they have Cypriot labour. Adrian has dozens of them working for him; men and women. Besides,' she added with some indignation, 'my brother wouldn't expect anyone to do two jobs for the price of one.' She shrugged. 'No, I can't think why he wants a man, and it doesn't really matter. But Mum is worried about it and you'll cheer her up no end. You will come?'

'Straight from work? I haven't brought my things with me.'

Josie glanced at her watch.

'Look, if you can swallow that in five minutes we'll just have time to go to the flat and pick up your nightie and toothbrush. Come on, don't be so staid!'

They were on the road just after five. Despite her normal frivolity of manner Josie was a good and steady driver and spoke little when in charge of the car. The car was large and luxurious; Mary sat back, relaxed, her wide eyes pensive and rather sad. Four years next week since it had happened. The whole scene came back; it always did at this time of the year.

She recalled once more the brusque and heartless way in which Vance had asked for the return of his ring.

Stunned, Mary had told him not to joke about such things while at the same time trying to fight against the terrible conviction that he was in deadly earnest. He was in love with her cousin, her seventeen-year-old cousin who had come over from Yorkshire to stay with Mary for a few weeks after recovering from an illness. Looking back, Mary felt she had become fully matured that day, had lost for ever the vivacity and lightheartedness which had made her the most popular girl in their crowd. She had stood so quietly, so gravely, facing Vance. Even though her heart was breaking she could not shed a tear.

'Give yourself time, Vance. It could be infatuation – and Betty, she's a mere child and can't know her own mind. Ours has been such a wonderful love affair, I can't believe you've stopped loving me. I know *I* shall never have anyone else.'

His face darkened; he too had spoken quietly, but Mary sensed the underlying fury, a fury born of guilt.

'It's over. I love her and I want to end our engagement. This is something beyond me – I can't help myself.'

But Mary had made him wait and in the end he'd promised to return in a week's time, when he had thought it over. If he still felt the same she would return his ring and never trouble him again.

Impossible now to imagine how she had lived through that week. And in the end he never came; he was in hospital, the promise of a brilliant career at an end.

'He'll need me now,' she had told her grandmother, with whom she lived. 'He won't want to break it off – he can't.'

'Are you resigned to being the wage-earner?' her grandmother had asked, shaking her head in doubt. 'Not much of a prospect for you, child.'

'I don't care. I loved him when he had a perfect body and I still love him. You don't change when misfortune strikes; you draw closer together. I'd have married him for better or worse. I still mean to marry him. There will be other things to make up for – for . . .'

'The things you can't do? You'll never have children, Mary. That won't satisfy a girl like you. You can't be willing to make such a sacrifice – nor be expected to. Look what you would miss.'

Mary would not listen. Vance needed her and she would

not fail him. She would try to make up in some small way for his terrible affliction. She didn't mind what she missed so long as Vance was there, by her side ... always.

'I still think you would be well advised to make a clean break. I can't last long— No, child, I feel it. And when I'm gone you can sell this place and get something smaller, perhaps a flat. You've a good steady job and you can carry on like that for a while. Eventually you'll meet someone else. Think over my words carefully, Mary. The life you contemplate is going to be one of much giving and very little taking. It won't work, my dear.'

Mary visited the hospital as soon as she was allowed. Grandmother did not understand. Mary knew she could be happy. She and Vance would make a new life, a different one from what they had planned. They'd study the arts, they'd become interested in music, there would be compensations in plenty. Yes, she could make him happy, and find happiness herself in doing so.

But Vance hadn't needed her, or so he had thought at the time. For no one had told him he would never walk again, that the best he could expect would be to move himself around in a wheelchair.

He lay there, his fair head against the pillow, looking up at Mary with a calm untroubled gaze. It was only a matter of weeks, he had told her, before he would be playing again. Betty and he would be married just as soon as he left hospital. And Mary had said, in an agony of despair,

'You'll need me, Vance, you don't know ...' She had tailed off; it was not for her to tell him. He'd be told only when he was in a fit condition to withstand the shock.

'Need you? What are you saying? Have you made up your mind to return my ring? I'll not feel free until I have it. You promised, and it's over a week. Give it to me!'

The nurse had found him, ten minutes later, unconscious, the ring clutched in his hand.

It had made a good story, the sort of story the press likes to publish. It was a scoop, a good follow-up after the headlines had splashed their news that the career of one of the country's most brilliant players had ended so tragically in a car crash. Perhaps the story was even more attractive, from a reporter's point of view, as it was only five months since the news of their engagement had hit the headlines.

On first reading of her supposed perfidy Mary had naturally been indignant and upset, but had resigned herself to a long wait before Vance could reveal the truth. For there were the operations, one after another, and Vance drugged for much of the time in between. Then came the shocked realization that Vance did not intend revealing the truth. Even then Mary forgave him, because of his suffering. The truth would come out eventually, when his engagement to Betty was announced, for surely he would then confess to what he had done. So Mary had borne the contempt of the neighbours and the loss of her friends stoically, feeling it was only a matter of time before they learned that the press had the story all wrong, learned that she had not jilted Vance because he would never walk again, had not returned his ring of her own accord, but had given it to him only when, after she had again hesitated, he had become almost hysterical. But the truth was never to come out. Betty took herself back to Yorkshire, disappeared before anyone had ever heard of her existence. At the same time everyone was commiserating with Vance, expressing sympathy, deploring Mary's action. Mary at last came to the conclusion that all this was balm to Vance at a time when he could be forgiven for accepting it. It satisfied a need, compensated in some small way for what he suffered. Mary could understand his reluctance to turn the tables on himself by owning to being the guilty party. Perhaps there had come a time when he would have liked to reveal the truth, but by then it probably seemed to Vance that it was too late, that there was nothing to be gained by bringing the incident before the public eye when it had long since been forgotten. But it had not been forgotten and it sometimes seemed to Mary that the fingers would point for the rest of her days. She had tried, only once, to vindicate herself.

13

The friend to whom she had revealed the truth had turned on her with scorn, saying she had never heard a story less convincing.

On her grandmother's death Mary thought of going right away, but she had a good post – at least, a well-paid post, but even Mr. Cartwright treated her with cold contempt, believing as he did that she had done that terrible thing to Vance.

The car came to a standstill, jerking Mary back to the present.

'Here already! You must have been speeding.'

'I thought you'd gone to sleep,' Josie grinned, 'so I never spoke a word.'

It seemed that the week-end was to pass just as pleasantly as the previous one had done. The dainty bedroom with its blue and gold bathroom adjoining was a real luxury. It was such a treat to lie in the bath without the continual rattling of the door handle telling her that she'd no right to be occupying the bathroom for so long. Those girls in the flat above seemed to spend half their lives in the bathroom. Then there were the brisk walks and the log fires, the meals prepared and put before her, with no dishes and messy pans to deal with afterwards. There were the long and intelligent conversations with Mrs. Stanning – with of course the interruptions of Josie's prattle every now and then. On the Saturday, though, Josie took herself off to a dance in town and Mary had a quiet evening with her hostess, talking and listening to the play on the radio.

The following afternoon Mary and Mrs. Stanning were in the sitting-room enjoying a quiet read before tea, when Josie came from the hall, a puzzled expression in her vivid blue eyes.

'That was Cleone on the phone, and she—'

'Cleone?' Mrs. Stanning glanced up sharply from her book.

'She wanted to know if you would be in this evening. I had to say yes, and she's coming round about eight.'

'Coming here?' Mrs. Stanning frowned heavily. 'What

can she want?'

Josie shrugged.

'Queer, isn't it? – after all this time. It can't be a social visit.'

'I didn't know she was in these parts. Where is she living?'

'She's on a visit to a friend, or so she said. But I gained the impression that she's around here simply because she wants to see you.'

Her mother fingered her book absently, a rather troubled expression on her face.

'I wish you'd put her off, dear. I've no wish to see Cleone, either this evening or at any other time.'

'I couldn't put her off, Mum. She took me by surprise and I said you were in and weren't thinking of going out this evening. In any case I couldn't have lied, could I?'

'No, dear, of course not.'

For the remainder of the afternoon Mrs. Stanning was silent and preoccupied, and it seemed as if that telephone call had put a blight on the rest of the day, for even Josie was not her usual bright and abandoned self. Mary suggested a walk after tea and to her surprise Mrs. Stanning declined. She loved walking and on previous occasions had been only too eager to accompany Mary through the fields or along the country lanes.

Josie came into Mary's bedroom as she was preparing to dress for dinner.

'You're ready!' gasped Mary. 'Is my watch wrong? Am I late?'

'I'm early for once; don't be alarmed, you have plenty of time.'

Mary was seated at the dressing-table, in a pale green negligée, very frilly and not what she usually wore. But Josie had almost bullied her into buying it when she was coming to The Wardens on her previous visit. Josie came and stood behind her chair and for a moment their eyes met in the mirror.

'Let me do your hair in a different style.' Josie picked

15

up the comb. 'We've been having lessons on how to make the most of our hair. Are you wearing the green, the one you wore last night?'

'It's the only one I have with me, so I've no choice.'

'It matches your eyes, in a way, but your eyes are a sort of grey-green, aren't they? They're a lovely colour, Mary, and your hair – russet, isn't it? I quite envy you.' She paused to look closely at her. 'Yes, you suit green, I knew it when I persuaded you to buy the negligée.' Josie began to comb through Mary's hair and for a while she concentrated on her task. 'If you've high cheekbones you should accentuate them by keeping the hair away, like that. If you've a wide forehead you can have a lock falling over. There!'

'It all sounds very technical, and rather complicated,' Mary laughed.

'It is. Much research has gone into this beauty business. I had no idea until I went to the school how much you can do to improve yourself ... not that *you* need. ...' Josie seemed to be speaking to herself; it was as if she had suddenly made a discovery. She finished her task, put down the comb and used her hands to pat the odd stray hair into place.

'Has anyone ever told you you're beautiful?' she asked, her hands still resting on Mary's head. A soft flush spread, but Mary did not speak, for a little ache had caught her throat. Vance had said all those things a girl in love wishes to hear. 'You're beautiful – with a difference,' went on Josie, and still Mary said nothing; she was startled to hear her friend so serious. 'Someone once said that no woman can possess real beauty until she has suffered. Have you suffered, Mary? But of course you have, losing your parents so young and then your grandmother. ...'

The conversation at dinner turned to Cleone, and after a while, feeling that their guest was being left out, Mrs. Stanning began to explain.

'Cleone – Mrs. Bostock – is Adrian's ex-fiancée.'

'Oh. ...' Mary darted a glance at her friend. Josie had told her a little about her brother but had made no mention of a fiancée. In fact Mary had formed the impression that he had never had any time for women, that he was a confirmed bachelor whose sole aim in life was the amassing of money. Her surprise brought forth some further explanation.

'It will be eight years ago now – Adrian was only twenty-three, and rather young for his age at that time. He knew his own mind, though, and there's no doubt that he loved Cleone deeply. We were all delighted with her – my husband was alive then – and thought her quite adorable. It's strange how a girl can appear so charming, so sincere and lovable, and yet hide her true nature. You see, Adrian met with an accident when out hunting; we were told he would lose his arm. At that time there seemed no hope of saving it. Cleone, who as I said, appeared to be the sweetest of girls, threw Adrian over even as he lay in hospital waiting for the operation. For a long while he wouldn't take it in and this made it difficult for us to comfort him. You see, Adrian has very definite ideas about love and marriage. His contention is that one's love should be strong enough to ride any misfortune. If it isn't strong enough then one should never have contemplated marriage in the first place. I think she did love him quite deeply, for she came to see me and wept bitterly. I'm sure she felt the loss, hated the thought of giving him up, but at the same time couldn't resign herself to marrying a man who was not perfect in body.'

'How awful!' exclaimed Mary, thinking of the way Vance's tragedy had made her feel closer to him than ever before. 'Your son was better off without her.'

'Indeed he was, but in his state of mind he didn't think so. He was very low; anyone would be low who expected to lose a limb at the age of twenty-three. And Adrian was so proud, so active in every way. I think only I, as his mother, can fully understand his agony of mind, but only he himself knows just what he went through, of course.' She gave a deep sigh and for a moment fell into reflective silence. 'It was a sad time for us all, but fortunately there came along a man who has since become a brilliant surgeon. He operated, three times, and now my son's arm is as good as ever – at least, almost as good as ever. It does cause him a little trouble now and then, but only if he's been overworking it.' She gave a slight grimace. 'On these rare occasions he becomes pretty difficult to live with.'

'That's an understatement,' flashed Josie, looking up to cast an almost accusing glance at her mother. 'You always did make excuses for him.' She turned to Mary. 'He gives everyone hell, and I really mean hell! He can't speak a civil word, even. Believe me, if you do come into contact with him when he's having trouble with his arm you'd declare him to be the rudest, most ill-mannered person you'd ever met.'

'No need to go off like that, dear. You don't understand, never having suffered such pain. You mustn't get the wrong impression, Mary. It's only when he's overtired, and that's not often.'

'It doesn't want to be,' declared Josie with some heat. 'And, anyway, how do you know how often it happens?'

Mrs. Stanning spoke to Mary, with that familiar mild and quiet inflection in her voice.

'As a matter of fact, the arm improves all the time; the doctor said it would be a long job, but eventually he would feel no pain at all. Adrian's trouble is that he tends to forget its limitations and sometimes overworks it. He's done that when he's been home on visits, and I get very cross with him about it.'

'I'll bet he's overworking it out there, and that all his poor slaves are squirming under that lashing tongue and wishing they didn't have to work for him.'

'Don't exaggerate so, Josie,' said her mother in the same mild tones. 'I'm quite sure dear Adrian is taking care and not working too hard. Didn't I write and ask him only a few weeks ago? And you remember that he replied saying he was doing exactly as I advised and taking plenty of rest?'

Josie, grinning, shot a significant glance at Mary, who had

to smile, though she was ca
see it. Her eyes strayed to th
graph in its lovely antique fr
do exactly as he pleased and
one else, told him to do. No d
man – if the photograph portr
inflexible mouth and stern col
lined and the brows faintly arch
peculiar mainly to the aristocracy
face and, for apparently no reason
eyes, trying to imagine what he looked
Perhaps he rarely did smile. Those strong silent men seemed
to consider it beneath their dignity to smile. She thought
of his agony when he believed he must lose his arm and
could imagine how his pride would suffer if his body were
not perfect. She could imagine too, the blow to his pride
on being jilted and wondered if he'd ever really recovered
from the humility of it.

'This Mrs. Bostock, what can she want—?' Mary broke
off in sudden confusion. What had made her say that? It
was none of her business.

'I cannot think, but, as we said, it is certainly not a social
call. She could be at a loose end, though,' Mrs. Stanning
added thoughtfully. 'Her husband died a few months ago and
she's been running round ever since visiting friends and
relatives. She can't seem to settle, from what I hear. Wasn't
happy with her husband, either, from all accounts.'

'Perhaps she wants to see Adrian again,' suggested Josie,
helping herself to vegetables. 'She might not know he's in
Cyprus.'

'She must do; certainly she'll know.' Mrs. Stanning spoke
sharply, and with an underlying note of anxiety. 'I
thought you said you had the impression she wishes to see
me – me particularly.' She paused. 'Cleone would never
have the nerve to try and contact Adrian again.' Once more
her tone held anxiety, fear even, thought Mary, watching
her take the vegetable dish from Josie. Then she handed it
to Mary. 'I'm not hungry; do help yourself, Mary dear.'

...ited to see you,' Josie put in. 'It was ... she might hope to see Adrian — because ... at she should come here. But don't look so ..., darling, Adrian wouldn't even look at her now.'
'...wonder. . . .' Mrs. Stanning turned to Mary. 'He ...ly did think a lot about her. After the medical treatment had ended he joined another man who was going to Cyprus to work some plantations there. Adrian now has his own groves and he's in big business, one of the island's largest exporters in fact. He seems content enough now, but I'm sure he went out to escape, because he couldn't trust himself to be sensible if Cleone should try to patch things up again. You see there's no doubt that had the positions been reversed Adrian's love for Cleone would have stood the test.'

'But he *has* made this new life for himself — he must have forgotten Mrs. Bostock, after all this time.' Mary spoke absently; she wasn't particularly interested in Adrian's past affair with Cleone, but she could understand Mrs. Stanning's anxiety and felt extremely sorry for her.

'He's made a new life — yes,' Mrs. Stanning agreed. 'And it would appear that he has forgotten her, for he's a very different man now from the unhappy boy who went over there eight years ago, a very different person from the one who loved Cleone, and yet. . . .'

'Yes?' It was Josie who spoke, regarding her mother with an odd expression. Once again she surprised Mary by her seriousness of manner.

'Well, do you remember what happened one time when he was over? Four years ago, it was,' she told Mary. 'And something occurred that made me wonder whether he still had some feeling for Cleone. Do you remember, dear,' she said to her daughter, 'that I passed a remark on it at the time? He had idly picked up our local paper and was reading about a girl jilting her boy — he was something in sport. . . .' She looked to Josie for help.

'A footballer. I don't know who because we don't take much interest in football,' she said, looking at Mary.

'No, and of course Adrian didn't know him either. But the case was very similar to his. The boy had met with an accident and the girl heartlessly threw him over when she learned he would never walk again. She actually gave him his ring back when he was in hospital. I am right in my facts, aren't I?' she asked her daughter.

'Yes. Gosh, was Adrian in a fury!' Josie actually shuddered. 'It was a quiet fury — almost terrifying, if you can imagine what I mean?'

Mary tried to swallow the hard lump in her throat; it was impossible, and she pushed her meat to one side of her plate. Her face had flamed and she dared not look up. Was there to be no escape? Would it be like this throughout her life? Surely there was some place where she could find peace, where her past would not follow her. After a little while she became more composed. Neither of her friends remembered, or were interested in, the names of the people concerned. They knew little about it apart from the main point, the similarity to Adrian's own case.

'Never have I seen my son so angry. It was as though he lived through the whole terrible business again. He said women like that weren't fit to live, that the girl ought to be strangled. The strength of his words and his outward show of emotion were so uncharacteristic that I couldn't help wondering if they hid something deeper, if he still had some love for Cleone.'

'If he felt anything I should think it would be hate,' interposed her daughter. 'It sounded like hate.'

'Perhaps; all the same, I'm glad he's so far away—'

'He'd never be willing to forgive her!' exclaimed Josie. 'I don't know what you're worrying about.'

'Well, I'll say again, I'm glad he's so far away.' She paused and Mary was startled by the sudden fire in her eyes. 'If I thought there was the slightest danger of their meeting again I'd stop at nothing to prevent it!'

'Does he know she's a widow?' Mary's eyes strayed to the photograph again. Despite her deductions regarding his character she knew he could love deeply, even as his mother said. Perhaps, then, he would be willing to forgive Cleone for what she had done to him all those years ago, when she was so very much younger.

'I don't think so. I have never told him and I don't expect Cleone would be so shameless as to write to him.'

Her eyes still on the photograph, Mary reflected again on the idea that Adrian would be willing to forgive. Hadn't she herself been only too willing to forgive Vance?

Yes, Mary could well understand Mrs. Stanning's anxiety, her grave concern at the possibility of a reconciliation if the two should meet again now that Cleone was widowed and free once more to marry.

CHAPTER TWO

THEY all went into the sitting-room after dinner and sat drinking coffee and chatting. Yet from the first there was a tenseness in the atmosphere and it was a relief to Mary when she heard a car draw up to a halt just outside the window.

She became conscious of the maid opening the door, of a softly-drawling voice; she became aware of the alertness of her friend, of the pulsating muscle in Mrs. Stanning's neck. She was like an animal poised for attack, yet at the same time quivering as if wary and on her guard.

Then the woman entered, tall and expensively tailored, her pale gold hair plaited round her head, gleaming and immaculate.

Mary gave a start as she interpreted the glance that Mrs. Stanning directed at her visitor. It held open hostility, and although it was feasible that such hostility existed, it surprised Mary that Mrs. Stanning would allow it to be revealed. She had struck Mary as a woman to whom politeness and good manners were all-important, a woman who at all times would contrive to keep her feelings hidden under a veneer of amiability. Mary received a further shock as, the introductions over, and when Cleone was reclining gracefully in a chair, Mrs. Stanning spoke again.

'I won't pretend that this is to be a friendly occasion, Mrs. Bostock. Why are you here?'

The gloves were to be off right away, it seemed.

Cleone appeared slightly disconcerted, but soon recovered. Mary felt she had never met anyone so confident or so beautiful.

'You know my husband died a short while ago?'

'I did hear something about it.' Mrs. Stanning's voice was cool and brusque.

'We were never happy – it was a mistake, my marrying him. When he died I kept on thinking of Adrian, and the feeling grew that I must see him again. Then I wondered if he were married, but none of my friends could tell me.' She paused and began smoothing her skirt with long slender fingers, keeping her eyes averted. 'However, three months ago I met a man who had just returned from Cyprus. He knew Adrian and told me that he had never even looked at a woman since going out there.' She gave Mrs. Stanning a direct and level glance, hesitating in order to allow the significance of her statement to sink in. 'There can be only one reason,' continued that smooth and confident voice. 'Adrian still cares for me.'

Becoming uncomfortable, Mary half rose, her lips forming an excuse to leave them to continue their conversation in private. But she was forced to sit down again as Mrs. Stanning began to speak.

'Please go on, Mrs. Bostock, we're extremely interested.'

Mary had to smile at her phrasing. She spoke like a queen. Nevertheless, there was a underlying lack of confidence in her manner. Mary had the impression that she felt trapped and that her brain worked furiously to devise some means of escape.

'I've known for some time that it was always Adrian – that I've never really ceased to love him. As it seems certain that he still loves me I feel that we can pick up the threads if only we can meet again.' She hesitated, a faint and strangely self-conscious smile touching her painted lips. 'But I'd no excuse for going over to Cyprus – I could scarcely just appear out of the blue and ask Adrian to take me back. I had to have a legitimate reason for going.' She looked at Mrs. Stanning, as if expecting some remark on that, but the older woman merely returned her stare, and waited. 'As you know,' Cleone went on, 'I was a secretary before my marriage, an efficient one, I believe—' She smiled again, faintly. 'I think I could measure up to Adrian's high standards.'

The little French clock on the mantelpiece was ticking far too fast, or so it seemed to Mary. It raced through the oppressive stillness of the room. She glanced up; a few minutes to nine.

'You've seen my advertisement – you did not notice I required a male secretary?'

'As you've been advertising so long I assume you're having difficulty. In view of this I feel sure Adrian will agree to employ a woman.' Cleone began smoothing her skirt again and Mary, moving her gaze to watch Mrs. Stanning's face, was amazed at the change in her expression. It was as if that last sentence had produced the germ of an idea – and that idea was growing rapidly. Mrs. Stanning no longer wore that trapped and desperate look. Her head came up with all the assurance of the victor. Having become more and more uncomfortable as the interchange continued Mary seized the opportunity of the lull and rose from her chair, saying,

'This is a private matter, Mrs. Stanning, I'll go into the other room.'

'Stay where you are.' Mrs. Stanning gave Mary a long deliberate stare, and then, slowly, 'After all, this does concern you, my dear.'

Startled into obedience, Mary sat down again with a little bump, at the same time darting a glance in Josie's direction. The younger girl's eyes widened; she was staring at her mother as if the most incredulous idea had crossed her mind. Mrs. Stanning said, with a sudden sweetness that seemed to conceal a virulent poison,

'So sorry for the interruption, Cleone. Do continue.'

'You must have reached the conclusion that it's impossible to find a male secretary for Adrian?'

'I have indeed.'

'So you agree with me that he'll be willing to employ a woman?'

'I do, Cleone.'

Cleone eyed her uncertainly and for a moment her confidence appeared to ebb.

'Well ... to come to the point, Mrs. Stanning, I'm applying for the post.'

A long silence. The smile of cool serenity that had

hovered on Mrs. Stanning's lips for the past moment or two slowly faded.

'Do you really believe, Cleone, that my son has been eating his heart out for you all these years?' She was playing, savouring some final blow. Mary caught her breath. There was a she-devil beneath the suave deceptive charm. She shivered, wondering what her son was like, Adrian, who she said took after her.

'Adrian loved me very deeply.'

'I agree. Adrian is like that.'

'And he hasn't married. . . .'

'My son is a very different person from the boy who loved you, Cleone,' said Mrs. Stanning after another silence. 'He's now a hard-headed business man, a man who does not appear to need a woman in his life. I believe he enjoys his bachelor existence, and is content to keep it that way.'

'I cannot agree.' Cleone stirred impatiently and a look of arrogance crossed her face. 'I'm applying for the post, but if you don't give it to me I shall not hesitate to go over to Cyprus and offer my services to Adrian myself. I think you'll agree there's no valid reason why I shouldn't apply for the post?'

The clock suddenly began to strike. Its soft and muted chimes which Mary had hitherto admired boomed like thunder through the stillness. Mrs. Stanning listened calmly for a while, and then,

'No reason at all, Cleone. But there is one good reason why I can't offer you the post. You see,' she added smoothly, 'it's already filled. Miss Roberts will shortly be going out to Cyprus as my son's secretary.'

The echo of the final chime dissolved into silence. It left the air electrified. Involuntarily, Mary tried to rise, but her body refused to move. She dared not look at Josie but was conscious of the little gasp being stifled by a swift raising of a hand to her mouth. Cleone became rigid and turned to look full at Mary, her dark eyes embers of smouldering hate. Shocked, Mary lowered her head, a strange and frightening sensation sweeping over her. Only Mrs. Stanning seemed totally unperturbed; she allowed her words to register more fully and then went on,

'So you see, Cleone, you're too late. Adrian is expecting Miss Roberts in a couple of weeks or so. I'm sure he'll be well satisfied with her work.'

No answer from Cleone. Mary raised her head to see the other woman regarding her intently. And then an odd light entered her eyes, and Cleone frowned in concentration.

'I've met you before,' she said, for the moment diverted.

'I'm sure we haven't met.' Mary examined her closely and shook her head. 'No, you're mistaken, Mrs. Bostock.'

Another long scrutiny, and again Mary experienced that peculiar sense of fear.

'Perhaps we haven't met, but ... I seem to know *of* you. Have you ever had your picture in the paper at all? Have you ever done anything that made news?'

Mary's lips became parched; she felt her heart throbbing with sickening speed as the other three awaited her reply.

'No – no, Mrs. Bostock, I – I've never done anything – newsworthy.'

'Odd, most odd. ... I wonder why I should have thought I'd met you – or seen your picture somewhere?' Her penetrating gaze continued to remain on Mary's face as if committing it to memory, and then, to Mary's intense relief Cleone shrugged, dismissing the matter. 'Oh, well, it isn't important.' Rising from the chair, she picked up her gloves. 'Accept my congratulations on your appointment. You're a lucky girl to be going out to such a beautiful island.' She had reached the door before Mrs. Stanning said,

'Josie dear, show Mrs. Bostock out. Josie, wake up! Show our visitor out.'

A good loser, concluded Mary as the door closed behind her. Losing the opportunity to contact Adrian again must have been a bitter blow, and yet she had accepted her fate so calmly. ... Mary's eyes suddenly flickered. To all outward appearances Cleone had accepted her fate calmly. ...

The front door closed. Mary listened for the car moving away, straining her ears for the final throb of the engine in the distance. But even as she waited for the last dying sound she again knew fear, and with that fear came the disturbing conviction that she had by no means seen the last of Cleone Bostock.

'Mother, what in heaven's name made you do a thing like that!' exclaimed Josie, dropping into a chair again on her return. 'And what a position to put poor Mary in. I think she was marvellous!'

Nothing marvellous about it, reflected Mary with an inward grimace. She'd been stunned into silence.

'I couldn't agree more.' Mrs. Stanning smiled across at Mary, but she spoke to Josie. 'Would you go and see about some coffee, dear, I'm sure we all need a drink. Make mine black – and strong.' When the door closed behind her daughter Mrs. Stanning turned again to Mary, holding her gaze steadily for a while before she said, 'Would you consider it, Mary? I shall be eternally grateful.'

Mary could only continue to stare. Mrs. Stanning, in desperation, had used her, but did she seriously believe she would do anything so impulsive as to throw up her job, leave her home, and go rushing off to Cyprus without giving the matter a moment's thought?

'Mrs. Stanning, I can't go off to Cyprus just like that.'

'Why not, dear?' asked Mrs. Stanning, mildly surprised. 'From what Josie tells me you haven't any close ties here, no relatives or—' She broke off, then continued, not in the least put out by her slip. 'We don't know anything about your private life, of course, but I gained the impression from Josie that you don't have ... a wide circle of friends.'

The slight hesitation spoke volumes. Mrs. Stanning was well aware that Josie was her only friend. And that friendship had puzzled Mrs. Stanning, judging by the surprise she had evinced on first being introduced to Mary. The difference in ages and personalities, Mary's quiet reserve and Josie's incessant chatter, even the difference in their choice of clothes. It was understandable that Mrs. Stanning should be surprised.

'It would be a wonderful change for you,' she went on, obviously interpreting Mary's silence as a sign of indecision, 'I can't understand why I never thought of it before—'

'But your son requires a male secretary. He'd scarcely welcome me—' Mary stopped. What was happening to her cautious, prudent mind? How came her thoughts to have escaped her strict control? 'I wouldn't consider taking up the post,' she stated on a firm decisive note.

'True, he did expressly ask for a man,' Mrs. Stanning agreed, apparently deaf to Mary's added statement. 'But I began to realize very soon that we weren't going to find anyone suitable. Men don't want these posts – I can't think why Adrian insisted on a man – one of his fads, evidently, but he's been without a secretary so long that he'll probably be tearing out his hair by this time, having to do all his own paper work in addition to everything else. No, my dear, I shouldn't worry about that. Adrian will welcome you with open arms.' She paused, for Mary was shaking her head emphatically. 'If you don't go Cleone will; that's what I'm afraid of, Mary, that's the real reason why I'm asking you.' She sounded almost desperate and Mary hastened to reassure her.

'Mrs. Bostock will hardly go after what you've just told her. She believes I'm engaged as Mr. Stanning's secretary and she has resigned herself to the situation.'

'She appeared to be resigned, but Cleone's no fool. She'll have been thinking, and I'll warrant she's already seen through my little game. Unless I'm much mistaken she'll make it her business to discover whether or not you go, and if you don't—' Mrs. Stanning shrugged as though half accepting defeat. 'Then she will, I'm very sure of that.'

Mary saw again the picture of Adrian Stanning and she spoke with conviction.

'Mrs. Stanning, if you'll excuse my saying so, I'm sure your son can handle his own affairs. Supposing Mrs. Bostock does go over to Cyprus; if Mr. Stanning wants her he'll have her, whatever your objections. And if he doesn't, he'll send her back to England. It's as simple as that.'

'It would be simpler still if they didn't meet at all.'

'Perhaps, but . . .' Once again Mary reflected on the possibility of his willingness to forgive. This of course was what his mother was afraid of. But if he were willing to forgive, if he did still care for Cleone, he certainly wasn't going to thank anyone for deliberately plotting to keep them apart. In fact, Mary felt convinced that even if he had no intention of taking Cleone back he would still be furious at the idea of anyone being so presumptuous as to try to arrange his life for him. 'I can't go,' she said again, aware that Mrs. Stanning was watching her closely as if searching for some sign of weakening. 'It's quite impossible.' Mary saw the shadow enter Mrs. Stanning's eyes and felt a growing sense of guilt; she was making an angry endeavour to shake it off when, to her relief, Josie came in with the coffee tray. No one spoke as Josie poured the coffee and it suddenly dawned on her that something was amiss.

'What's wrong, Mary, you look so pale.' She handed Mary her drink. 'Haven't you recovered from the shock yet?'

'Oh, yes, it isn't that.' Mary spoke without thinking and regretted it instantly as Josie's expression changed to one of inquiry.

'I've been trying to persuade Mary to accept the post of secretary to Adrian,' Mrs. Stanning submitted as Mary made no effort to explain. 'Unfortunately she feels she can't do it.'

'It's just that – that I couldn't uproot myself so – so suddenly. . . .' Mary tailed off, shaking her head. She began sipping her coffee as the feeling of guilt swept over her again.

'Of course she couldn't, Mother; you've no right to expect. . . .' Josie's voice trailed off to a murmur. Then her blue eyes suddenly sparkled. 'Why not?'

Mary blinked and then, noticing the laughing mischief in her friend's expression,

'Now, Josie, don't you try—'

'Why can't you go to Cyprus? What's stopping you, tell me that?' And, without waiting for an answer, 'All you have to do is give old Cartwright a week's notice — and your landlady. I'll miss you, but it will be a wonderful break for you. Come on, snap out of it. Oh, my staid Mary, your mother must have known when she christened you! Stop looking so horrified and do something impulsive for once in your life!'

'But it's ridiculous!'

'Why is it?' Josie poured her mother's coffee and handed it to her. 'Give me one good reason why you can't go?'

'Well . . . to throw up my job. . . .' Heavens, was she really contemplating so precipitate an action? One good reason, Josie had asked for. 'You implied that your brother would be a most difficult employer,' she submitted in a rather feeble protestation.

'Oh. . . .' Josie dismissed that with an airy gesture of her hand. 'It's only when he's been overworking, as Mum says. And it's only really with me — when he's at home, that is — because he thinks I'm flighty; but he'll take to you, with your efficiency and your tidy, methodical way of going about things.' She passed her mother the biscuits, then held out the plate to Mary. 'Think of the climate — all that gorgeous sun! You'll love it. Mum and I went over last year and we had a wonderful time. And the people; it's fun meeting new people.'

New people . . . people who would not treat her with contempt, who would not turn away or cross to the other side of the street when they saw her approaching.

'Josie's right, you would love the island,' Mrs. Stanning interposed in a soft, persuasive tone. 'And if you're at all travel-minded it's a most convenient centre.'

Mary was being pushed along, and after several rather half-hearted attempts to voice another protest she gave up and sat listening to what the others had to say.

There were the mountains and valleys and the wide spreading downlands; there were the beaches and the forests, the breathtaking spectacle of flower-clothed hills in spring, and the golden-tinted vine plantations in the winter. There were the ancient castles and monasteries, and even more ancient sanctuaries.

'You'll have no end of places to visit,' said Josie, carried away now by enthusiasm. 'Just think, your life won't be dull any more.' She paused, and her eyes lit again with mischief. 'You might even find yourself a husband, for Cyprus is "Love's Island", you know. Aphrodite, the goddess of love and all that,' she added teasingly. 'Rose from the foam off the coast of – somewhere or other.'

'Paphos, dear. Don't you remember, Adrian took us there?'

And so it continued, each adding their inducements, and each for their own reasons; Josie laughing and urging her to 'do something impulsive', but her mother much more serious in her aim.

For Mary to thrust out the idea soon became an impossibility; the promise of beginning a new life was far too attractive.

The tragedy had cast a shadow over her life for the past four years; she now had the chance of leaving it behind, of readjusting and making new friends. Her employer, she felt, would be even more formidable than the testy and irate Mr. Cartwright, but, knowing nothing of her past, he would be sure to extend to her a certain amount of civility and respect. Her thoughts reverted for a moment to what Vance's mother had once said, in tones of terrible bitterness.

'I expect you'll run away, but this will follow you. It will follow wherever you go!'

Well, it could scarcely follow her to Cyprus. There'd be no one over there to despise her, to treat her with the scorn and contempt she had had to endure since the day Vance had forced her to return his ring.

CHAPTER THREE

IT seemed, however, as if Mary were not to make a new life for herself in Cyprus after all, for everything went wrong from the first.

Adrian was not at the airport to meet her and Mary, travel-weary and feeling thoroughly lost and alone, stood by her luggage wondering what she should do. But soon her innate common sense came to her aid and she set about finding a taxi. There must be some good reason for her new employer's non-appearance; a mix-up in the date, perhaps, or the car could have broken down. The obvious course was to make her own way to his house.

With the kindly help of an airport official she was soon on her way. The taxi driver, a Turkish Cypriot, chatted all the time, telling her she must call him Selim. Like all Cypriots he was justly proud of his island and expounded on its beauties. He wanted to know if this was Mary's first visit, and when she told him it was he bade her welcome and went on to describe the interesting places she must see.

He was so friendly that before very long Mary had told him of the reason for her coming to the island. He knew Mr. Stanning, yes, very well, for he sometimes used the taxi to and from the airport.

'He travel to Israel and Egypt,' he went on, taking a narrow bend at a perilous speed. 'So he hire my taxi. You ... go to work for him, then?' A frown appeared, but only briefly. 'Look at the little horse! He wear the plumes – pretty, no? And the beads. ...' Selim rolled his eyes and continued to watch the horse, drawing a small open carriage. Mary held her breath, wondering how long he could drive without returning his glance to the road. 'The blue beads – you see them? They keep away the Evil Eye. Always they wear them, to send off the bad luck.' He leant forward, reaching to the back of the parcel shelf. 'I give you the beads – and you have always of the good luck, yes?'

'Thank you!' The beads were brilliant turquoise; Mary held them in her hand for a moment before putting them away in her bag. Although far from being superstitious, she felt strangely happy at the taxi driver's action. 'It's kind of you; I'll keep them always.'

His pleasure was instantly reflected in his smile, and Mary felt she had made her first new friend.

Adrian lived in Varosha, the new part of Famagusta, which was occupied mainly by Greeks, for the Turkish community were settled in the old walled city, a mile or so to the north.

The road from Nicosia traversed the Messaoria, an almost treeless plain that lay between the two great mountain ranges, the Kyrenia Range to the north and the Troodos Mountains to the south.

'In summer this is – what you say? – a desert,' the taxi driver told Mary. 'It is so hot, and parched. But now, with the winter rains over, it is growing the grain – very much grain we have. It grow fast in our beautiful sunshine.'

Mary looked through the open window of the taxi, gazing around her at the emerald fields, cropped with barley and wheat and splashed with all the glorious colours of spring. There were the reds and yellows of ranunculi, the brilliant scarlet of poppies and the purples and subtle mauves of anemones, irises and the exquisite little ground orchids. What a contrast to England at this time of the year. In early March one could expect only frost and biting winds, rain and mists and heavy clouds that made one feel the sun just couldn't be up there at all.

They were driving seawards across the plain, and here and there Mary caught sight of a little mud-hutted settlement and sometimes a slender minaret would rise above the dome of a Mohammedan mosque. Gradually the air became heady, charged with the sweet fragrance of orange blossom, for the groves covered miles of the countryside around Famagusta. There was a tang of the sea in the air, too, as they drove along a road bordered by giant eucalyptus trees

34

that provided a welcome shade from the increasing brilliance of the sun. This road connected the old and the new parts of the city and soon they had reached their destination.

The house was long and low and gleaming white with pale blue shutters; above some of the windows gay tasselled sun-blinds hung down to shade the rooms within.

Selim opened the door and Mary stood by the taxi, spellbound. Never had she seen such masses of flowers; everywhere the garden blazed with them; mimosa and bougainvillea, roses and wistaria; while along the borders were lemon and orange trees, waving palms and walnuts and cypresses.

'I will take your luggage,' said Selim as Mary, in a rather dazed manner, stooped to pick up one of her suitcases. 'This is the way.' Mary followed him, her interest in the house and the gardens evaporating as her mind began to dwell anxiously on the coming interview with her new employer which, she felt, would be far more difficult than the casual meeting that would have occurred had he met her at the airport. An actual interview had always held terrors for her and she often wondered if that were one of the reasons why she had never thought of leaving Mr. Cartwright.

The door was opened by a stout woman to whom Selim spoke in Greek. His smile began to fade as she replied to his question.

'Anya – she have no instructions about you,' he said, turning again to Mary. 'Mr. Stanning, he always so busy – he not remember to tell Anya—'

'Isn't Mr. Stanning here?'

'Not till this evening. He is at the office, down by the plantation.' He turned as the woman spoke. 'Anya say you leave your luggage here. Then I take you to Mr. Stanning, yes?'

He drove some distance and eventually they were travelling along a wide path, with the orange trees stretching away on both sides as far as the eye could see, and the air heavy with their scent.

35

The office, a white, modern building, stood at the far end of the grove. Selim brought the taxi to the front of the building and opened the door for Mary to get out.

'I show you where Mr. Stanning is? I take you to him?' he offered, and Mary thanked him gratefully. She wished she could have freshened up, for obviously she was to have a formal interview. Still, Mr. Stanning would understand and make allowances for her rather travel-stained appearance.

Selim took her right up to the door; it stood ajar and he pushed it further open. He smiled again and left her.

Mary knocked softly and went in, stepping on to the deep, thick carpet. Adrian Stanning sat at his desk, absorbed in some papers. His attitude of preoccupation appeared to exclude all else, for he never even looked up as Mary entered.

She stood by the door, taking in the whole scene in one all-embracing glance – and gasped in disbelief. The desk was piled high with papers; some of the correspondence was unopened. Every drawer in the filing cabinet was flung wide and its contents scattered about; even the waste-paper basket overflowed. What chaos! Where would she begin?

Her gaze returned to the man in the chair. He looked exactly as his photograph had portrayed him, but very tired. There were little grey lines at the corners of his eyes, and his left arm lay along the desk as if for rest or ease. Mary gave a small cough; his head came up with a jerk and his brows lifted a fraction. He stared at her blankly and waited for her to speak.

Mary was seized with nervousness, but she shook it off, anxious to give a favourable impression.

'Mr. Stanning?' She forced a smile, hoping she sounded brighter than she felt. 'I'm Mary Roberts, your new secretary.' She moved closer to the desk and stood there, her hands demurely clasped in front of her.

'My—!' He seemed speechless for a moment. 'You're my – *what*?'

Taken aback, Mary darted a glance at the desk with its

mass of unopened correspondence.

'Your – secretary. . . .'

'Are you indeed? This is the first I've heard about it.'
His voice was curt and low; his eyes retained their blank
expression.

'Didn't your mother let you know I was coming?'

His brow contracted.

'My mother had instructions to engage me a male secretary.'

'Yes; she advertised for one and—'

'And you applied?' He leant right back in his chair, tilting it on two legs, and regarded her in amazement. 'You
actually answered an advertisement that specifically stated
a man was required!' His voice echoed his incredulity.
'What sort of recommendation is that to a prospective employer? I can't think what possessed my mother even to
grant you an interview—'

'I didn't reply to the advertisement,' interrupted Mary,
going red. 'I happen to be a friend of your sister and that's
how I came to be offered the post.'

'That's even less of a recommendation. Josie hasn't a
brain in her head!' He swept her a glance of disdain. 'How
you came to persuade my mother to engage you is quite
beyond me.'

'I didn't persuade her.' Just the reverse, reflected Mary,
trying to suppress her indignation. 'But only two men applied and neither was suitable. So she thought you might
be glad of – be satisfied with a woman secretary.' Could
anything have been put more clumsily? Mary wondered
with growing dismay. It was understandable that he should
sit there, regarding her with such astonishment. 'It was
worrying Mrs. Stanning – having such difficulty,' she ended
lamely.

'Perhaps . . . but for your part, it was most rash of you
to come over here knowing full well that I wanted a man.'
He suddenly winced and began rubbing his left arm below
the elbow. 'Did it not occur to you that the sensible
course would be to write and find out whether or not I'd

be willing to employ a woman?'

Mary bit her lip and had to admit that the idea had not occurred to her. But she could not embark on any full explanation, or mention the urgency without involving his mother, and revealing her intention of keeping him and Cleone apart at all costs. He winced again and a scowl darkened his stern set features. 'Do you realize what inconvenience you've caused me? I shall have to waste my time arranging for your return flight! My sincere hope is that there'll be a seat on tomorrow's plane!'

Her heart sank. Would he not even give her an opportunity of demonstrating her efficiency?

'I've come all the way from England, Mr. Stanning,' she began persuasively, watching his scowl deepen. His arm was clearly giving him trouble, for although he no longer rubbed it, his eyes had assumed that faintly glazed look that comes with acute pain.

'Then you can go back to England, just as soon as I can arrange it. You're a damned nuisance— And my mother will hear from me about this!'

Mary's lips quivered and for a moment she couldn't speak. It was not merely the indignity of being packed off home that worried her, but also the prospect of readjustment, of finding a new post and a flat. Her eyes pricked and when at last she did manage to speak her tone was low and pleading.

'I've given up my job and my home. . . .'

'You can hardly blame anyone else for that,' he said relentlessly. 'If you've no more sense than to act in this rash and thoughtless manner you must be prepared to take the consequences. Certainly I can't be held responsible for any losses you've incurred. What would you have me do? Employ you out of a sense of chivalry? You can think again, my girl!' His words flicked, and hurt. Mary's eyes filled up; she lowered her head and rapidly blinked away the tears. 'I must add,' he went on, 'that this sort of behaviour is what I would expect from a girl who admits to being a friend of my sister. It's exactly what I would expect from

Josie herself.'

A long silence. Mary looked down at her hands, feeling like a child being chastised – and justly so. She *had* acted without thought. It had been an irresponsible act to throw up everything and come out here, knowing that he had expressly asked for a man. True, Mrs. Stanning had engaged her, and Mary had expected she would have notified her son. Something had certainly gone amiss there. But in any case the prudent and businesslike course would have been to wait for the reply stating whether or not he would consider employing a woman secretary. Almost defeated, she looked up, to stare at him miserably. So much for her hopes of escape, of forgetting the past and making a new life. And yet she had confidence in her abilities. Despite his opinion of her as a woman, her previous employer had done his utmost to persuade her to stay. Mary decided to make one final effort.

'If you would give me a trial, Mr. Stanning, I think – I think you might find me satisfactory.'

'Give you a trial?' His dark brows lifted. 'I require efficiency and dependability – which I consider not unreasonable. Your thoughtless and improvident action in coming here certainly does not indicate that you possess those qualities; quite the contrary, in fact.' He paused, allowing that to sink in, and Mary's lips curved bitterly. It was ironical that Josie's one complaint had been that she was too efficient and methodical. 'By your own admission you're impulsive, you act without caution or thought – and ask me to employ you? No, Miss Roberts, even if I were considering employing a woman I wouldn't for one moment entertain you. However, if it's any consolation to you, I'm not prepared to employ a woman. I've had enough of them. They come out here for excitement, to escape from their self-inflicted boredom. Serious work is the last thing they have in mind. They've read about – or heard about – the climate and the sea. They have no intention of settling; it's merely a break, an escape from routine—' His eyes roved over her, then rested on her face.

'From the way in which you've acted I don't doubt that you've come out here for a similar reason,' and when Mary blushed and lowered her eyes, 'I thought so. Was it routine from which you were trying to escape – monotony? – or was it something else? No, don't trouble to answer; I'm not interested. This is a complete waste of my time – and all so unnecessary. Why do women have to act with such lack of foresight!' He appeared to be finished with the matter; his attention turned once more to the paper in which he had been so absorbed when her entry had interrupted him. Mary moved uncomfortably, reluctant to speak; but obviously she couldn't just stand there, so she asked if he could tell her what she must do, where she must stay the night.

'At my home, I suppose,' he snapped, and then, his brow contracting. 'Where were you expecting to stay?'

'Your mother – Mrs. Stanning said she had informed you of my coming, and asked you to accommodate me temporarily until I could look round and find a suitable place to live.'

His lips compressed. It looked very much as if his mother would hear from him about that suggestion, too.

'I'll get someone to take you in the jeep. Anya, my housekeeper, will show you a room; I'll ring and give her instructions.'

The room looked out to a far sandy beach and the sea, but Mary had no interest in the view. She sat down on the bed and it was all she could do to suppress the tears. For the first time in her life she had acted without caution and this was the result. What was she to do now? After a few moments of determined effort to think clearly she put the matter from her, refusing to dwell on the future and the reorganization of her life. She surmised that there would be an offer of temporary accommodation at The Wardens until she could decide what she would do, and for the present Mary left it at that, being wise enough to own that she was in no fit state to cope with the confusion into which, through her precipitate action, she had landed herself. She was tired and dejected and humiliated, and that was quite enough to occupy her for the time being.

Anya had said that a meal would be ready at eight o'clock; Mary didn't know whether she would be invited to dine with Adrian, but if she was she had no intention of letting him see just how miserable he had made her feel. So, shaking off a little of her dejection, she unpacked a bright flowered linen dress, shook the creases out as best she could, and laid it on the bed. Then, after taking a quick refreshing shower she put on the dress, applied a little make-up, and brushed her hair. A final glance in the mirror satisfied her that she looked cool and presentable, and a little of her confidence returned as she went downstairs and into the room which Anya had told her was the dining-room.

Adrian Stanning was already there. His eyes, cool and impersonal, seemed to flicker over her without seeing her. She had the impression that although he knew he must endure her presence he intended to ignore it.

The meal was the most unpleasant Mary had ever taken. He obviously had no intention of carrying on a conversation with her, or of trying to put her at ease. What a rude, unsociable man he was! True, he was in some considerable pain with his arm, but that was no excuse for this churlish attitude, this complete lack of good manners. But perhaps she should be grateful for his silence, she thought, bringing to mind Josie's assertion that, when the arm was troubling him, he gave everyone hell. Yes, she decided, that interview could have been far more unpleasant, too. Presumably she had been lucky, for he had kept his temper in check, though not, she felt sure, because of her friendship with Josie, but owing to her acquaintanceship with his mother.

Immediately the meal ended she murmured an excuse and went to her room. Thoroughly exhausted, she was soon in bed and slept right through until eight o'clock the following morning. This astonished her since she had expected to be kept awake by anxiety. Grateful for the rest, which had left her wonderfully refreshed, she washed and dressed and went downstairs where, to her relief, she breakfasted alone. Then, wondering how to pass the time, she went into the garden and sat down in the sunshine, admiring the flowers. The house was on the edge of the town, with the orange groves behind and a view of the sea in front. All was still and quiet; the faint breeze coming in from the coast picked up the fragrance of some sweet-scented herb and wafted it through the air. The scent of roses, too, mingled with the perfumed air, coming from the low wall where the roses clambered luxuriantly over it, and from the nearby arbour where they splashed their colours against the emerald back-cloth of the cypress trees. Now and then Mary's attention was caught by the swift darting of a lizard between the gleaming limestone of the rockery.

She could have stayed, savouring the stillness, but anxiety made her restless and eventually she left the garden with the intention of exploring her immediate surroundings. She had not proceeded far, however, when panic overcame her and she hastened back to the house. If Adrian Stanning had managed to arrange a flight for today he would be far from pleased if she missed it.

Anya met her as she made to enter the house. Had she seen Mr. Stanning? He'd been back in the jeep and had asked for her. Mary stared at the woman in consternation.

'Didn't he leave a message?'

'Message?' Anya's brow furrowed. 'What is this – message?'

Mary began to explain and eventually Anya understood. No message had been left for her; Mr. Stanning had been extremely annoyed at finding her absent and had – from the way Mary interpreted Anya's words – stormed out and driven away in a cloud of dust.

'The jeep, you not see it for this – this dust, you know. It come up in the air – oh, all over this place!'

After standing uncertainly outside the office door for what seemed an eternity, Mary at last gathered the courage to knock. The words which reached her were Greek, but

42

she assumed they conveyed an invitation to enter, which she did, her mouth going dry when she saw Adrian Stanning's expression as he looked up and saw who it was. Judging by the way the papers on the desk were scattered, he had been searching hastily for something.

'Did you wish to see me?' she ventured, her glance once again taking in the state of the room. Even in her anxiety her mind rebelled at the scene of disorder around her.

'Where the devil have you been?' he demanded, glaring at her. 'I expected you to keep to the house? I've no time to career round the countryside looking for you!'

'I'm sorry ... I didn't go far. You've arranged for my return?'

'There's no seat available for a week – *now that you've missed today's flight*—'

'Oh, *no*! I'm terribly sorry, Mr. Stanning.' Mary looked straight at him, her distress evident. 'Can't I catch the plane, if I hurry? My things are packed. ...' She tailed off as an angry exclamation left his lips.

'This is a damnable inconvenience for me! And if it's an example of the consideration you extended to your former employer, then he must have accepted your resignation with the utmost alacrity!'

The unfairness of that brought a lump to Mary's throat; she found her hands were twisting nervously together and put them behind her back.

'I'm so sorry,' she said again, and then, rather helplessly, 'What shall I do now?'

Again he glared at her.

'I don't care what you do so long as you don't expect me to entertain you!' He began searching among the papers again, every movement reflecting his impatience. He stopped, to press the fingers of his right hand soothingly into his left wrist. Mary glanced round again, coughed nervously and then,

'Now that I'm here for – for a week, perhaps I can be of some assistance.' She noticed a letter in the typewriter; on the desk at the side was a rough draft from which he had obviously been working. 'Can I re-type this letter for you?'

'What do you mean, re-type? It only requires to be finished.'

Mary took in the several typing errors.

'Then perhaps I can finish it for you?' she amended diplomatically. And she added, noticing that he still held his wrist, 'Whatever you've lost . . . I may be able to find it, if you tell me what it is.'

A biting refusal undoubtedly rose to his lips, but before he could utter it his eyes darkened with pain and he said, though not at all graciously,

'Yes, you can finish the letter. And the papers I'm looking for are in a folder – a brown folder; they're important as I need them this afternoon.' He paused as if reluctant to continue speaking in this civil tone to her, but perhaps her contrite expression had some favourable effect because he continued, rising from his chair, 'I'm going home now to change; I've a meeting at two-thirty with several business associates. If you can find that folder it will save me a deal of trouble.' He picked up a briefcase and crossed to the door. 'And don't touch anything else,' he warned. 'I know where everything is.'

'You . . .?' Discreetly she stopped, but she couldn't do anything about the wide stare of amazement that entered her eyes.

He flashed her an arrogant glance and went out.

When the letter was re-typed Mary cleared the blotter and laid the letter there for Adrian to sign. Then she set about seaching for the folder. It seemed an impossible task. How could he have managed to get the place into such a mess? she wondered, and recalled Mrs. Stanning's saying that he would probably be tearing out his hair, having to do all his own paper work in addition to everything else. She also recalled, not without bitterness, that his mother had been very sure he would receive her 'with open arms'.

The brown folder was wedged above one of the drawers in the desk; Mary had found it quite by chance when trying to close the drawer and its discovery gave her an inordinate sense of satisfaction. For she was strongly of the opinion that failure on her part would have resulted in her dropping even lower in Adrian Stanning's estimation. Not that she could fall much lower, she owned to herself with a sigh of dejection as she turned to go.

Again her instinct rebelled at leaving the place in this state of confusion and she came back into the room. Mindful of his injunction not to interfere with anything else, Mary at first contented herself with picking up the papers lying on the floor, but then she began to tidy the desk. The sorting of the papers entailed filing them, and so it went on until the whole place was tidied up. She was wondering where she could find a brush or cleaner for the carpet when there came a knock at the door. Mary opened it to find one of the workers standing there. He spoke little English, but she was able to understand that he wanted to see Mr. Stanning. As he did not seem particularly disappointed at his failure to see him, Mary concluded that whatever he wanted could not be very important. She then asked about the cleaner, and also indicated the waste-paper basket.

'Where can I empty that? Do you know?'

He grinned amicably and led her through the outer office and along a passage. He took out the cleaner from a cupboard in the wall. Then he offered to dispose of the rubbish for her.

'No, I'll do it.' She wanted first to examine the contents of the basket. 'Just show me where to put it.'

After cleaning the carpet and giving the room a thorough dusting Mary emptied the contents of the basket on to a piece of paper. Just as she had guessed; an important-looking document and an unopened letter.

And he had baldly announced that he knew where everything was!

A tinge of disappointment mingled with her satisfaction as, her task finished, she stood looking round. She had half expected to find Mrs. Stanning's letter among the unopened correspondence, but long before she had finished her task she recalled that Josie had offered to post the letter. . . .

She heard Adrian Stanning enter the outer office. Undoubtedly she would be taken to task for her trouble, but she was past caring. Nevertheless, her pulse did quicken as she turned to face him. Pausing by the door for a time, he coolly surveyed the room, then his gaze settled on Mary; a searching gaze with a spark of anger that threatened to explode. Mary steeled herself, but he jerked his head towards the desk and whatever he had intended saying was checked.

'You found the folder, then?'

'It had become caught above one of the drawers in the desk.'

Approaching the desk, he picked up the document she had taken from the waste-paper basket.

'Where did you find this? I've been searching everywhere for it.'

'It was . . . about,' she returned, very sure that nothing would be gained by telling him the truth. 'This letter came to light at the same time.'

Judging by the way he picked it up and scrutinized the letter Mary conducted that its loss, too, had caused him some inconvenience, but he made no comment on that. She received no thanks for tidying up the room, but neither was rebuked for doing so. Glancing at the clock he said,

'Have you had any lunch?'

'I'm not hungry.'

'It's two o'clock; you must be. Go back to the house and ask Anya to get you something.'

'It doesn't matter, Mr. Stanning, I can wait until tea time.'

'As you wish,' he said indifferently, and sat down at his desk.

At dinner that evening there seemed to be more flexibility in his attitude towards her, but despite this her dejection grew, for there was no indication that he would relent, and throughout the meal his tones remained curt and precise. Nevertheless he did make some effort to converse, asking Mary about his mother and Josie. Mary soon gath-

ered that in spite of his earlier disparaging reference to his
sister's behaviour he did possess an underlying affection for
her. As the meal progressed the conversation flagged and
once again Mary sighed with relief when at last she was able
to leave the table and go to her room, where she sat for a
time, trying to read. This being impossible, she put on a
coat and went out to the garden.

The night was warm and balmy, the garden silver-misted
under the star-laden eastern sky. The air was heady with the
lingering fragrance of lavender and wild thyme. Mary
wandered along a narrow winding path, overhung with tall
shrubs which shut out the stars. Emerging at the other end
she was delighted with the little arbour confronting her. A
rustic garden seat invited and she sat down, soothed by the
stillness and the isolation.

Footsteps intruded into her calm and Adrian Stanning
came into the arbour. He stopped, plainly surprised.

'So you've found my little retreat, Miss Roberts.'

She stood up, glad of the dimness that hid her rising
colour.

'I'm sorry.' Mary fingered the ends of her hair with a
little nervous gesture she had when at a disadvantage or
when she was ill at ease. 'I'm just going.'

'There's no need.' He sat down. 'Stay by all means, if you
like.' He sounded more amicable and Mary wondered
if his arm were easier now. 'I must thank you for finding
those papers for me, Miss Roberts,' he went on, surprising
her still further. 'They contained information which was
of vital importance to the success of my meeting.' He
did not expand on that and the silence dropped again.

'If you'll excuse me,' said Mary at last, getting up, 'I
think I'll go to bed.' She could have stayed, had he not
been there, but her stupidity in coming here, and the humiliation resulting from it, hung over her like a cloud; she
felt she could never be comfortable in Adrian Stanning's
presence again.

'Certainly, but as I said, there's no need to run away on
my account.' His tones were curt but plainly sincere.

47

'I . . . well, it is a beautiful evening.' Mary hesitated, then sat down again, on the edge of the seat. 'We're having a very cold spell in England just now,' she added conversationally.

'So I believe.'

From far out at sea the lights of a ship flickered; the new moon, a thin crescent, seemed to hang alongside it. For a little while calm enveloped Mary again, and then she said awkwardly,

'What day do I – do I leave?'

'Wednesday – a week tomorrow.' A pause. 'What are you going to do with yourself?'

Was he really interested? – or merely making conversation? Whatever the reason for his question, it surprised her.

'I don't know.' She half turned, an involuntary movement, and gave him a wan little smile. 'I suppose I should make the most of it and see something. Selim – the taxi driver – told me of some places to visit.' Not much fun on her own, she thought despondently. That was the reason she had always kept to the flat, preferring her books and records to wandering about by herself. Adrian remained silent and after a little while Mary said, hesitantly, 'If I could be of some use to you, I really would be glad to help.' Her eyes sought for the ship again, a vague silhouette poised on the dark horizon.

'What do you expect to achieve by that?' inquired Adrian on a cool sardonic note.

Mary replied bleakly,

'Nothing, Mr. Stanning. I know you would never employ me permanently.'

A faint breeze fluttered, sprinkling the air with new and heady perfumes. The sky had darkened to a deep purple, rich and velvet-smooth. England seemed a million miles away.

'Why did you come?' was the next and totally unexpected question. He crossed one leg over the other and Mary noticed that it was in order to provide a support for

48

his arm.

Again her voice contained that bleak little accent.

'There were several reasons, I admit, but—' She turned with that swift, involuntary gesture, this time as if to emphasize her words. 'Contrary to your opinion of me, I did come out prepared for work.'

'Is that what you want, then? – to spend these next few days working?'

'I should be bored otherwise – the time would drag, I'm sure.'

'Very well, Miss Roberts, but,' he added warningly, 'don't indulge in any false optimism. I meant what I said about not employing another woman.'

Never had Mary been driven at such a pace. She suspected she was pulling up weeks of neglected work, and yet she felt that Adrian Stanning had some other reason for working her so hard. The idea did occur that he was testing her, but she dismissed it, sure that he remained adamant about sending her home.

On the Monday afternoon he brought in a great sheaf of papers and threw them on to Mary's desk.

'All these figures have to be amended,' he said. 'And it's imperative that they're finished by Wednesday afternoon. If you'll make a start and do as much as you can I'll finish them myself.'

Although staggered by the amount of work involved, Mary tackled it methodically and even surprised herself by the speed with which she was getting through it. However, by lunch time on Tuesday she realized there would still be a large proportion left unfinished, for as her flight was scheduled for ten o'clock on Wednesday morning, she could not work at all on that day.

On sudden impulse she decided to make a concentrated effort to finish the work herself, for she could see Adrian sitting up all night in an effort to complete it. She worked right through her lunch hour, stopping only for a cup of coffee in the afternoon when Adrian had his; by five o'clock she was exhausted, but still determined to carry on.

Adrian came out of his office and stood beside her chair, watching her work for a moment or two, then he picked up the stack of papers lying on the desk and scanned the top sheet. He didn't look at any of the others and Mary found herself strangely gratified, for it seemed that he had confidence that the work had been carried out efficiently.

'You've broken its back,' he said in tones less curt than those with which she had become familiar. 'The rest can be left till the morning.'

'No, you wouldn't get through it, Mr. Stanning; there's still a great deal to be done.'

'I'm not going home myself for another hour or so,' he told her, ignoring her comments. 'But I've sent for someone to run you back now. Have a rest before dinner, a lie down. You'll be surprised how refreshed you'll feel.' The inexorable tone should have warned her not to argue, but she hated the idea of leaving the work unfinished.

'I really can carry on. I shouldn't feel satisfied if I left it now.' An uncomfortable silence followed her words; she sensed it even before she turned to the typewriter again to resume her work. Her fingers hesitated on the keys; she looked up to meet the arrogant stare of those intensely dark and penetrating eyes.

'Miss Roberts,' said Adrian softly, 'I don't permit my employees to argue with me.' Mary blinked at him, her eyes glistening with hope, but the question stuck in her throat and before she could voice it one of the men appeared in the open doorway. 'Take Miss Roberts home,' he said. 'Use the jeep.'

'The jeep, she is up the field.'

'Then take my car ... and don't drive on your brakes, understand?'

'Yes, sir!' he grinned. 'I drive your car with the very great care.'

'You'd better,' warned Adrian, and returned to his own office.

In less than half an hour Mary was on the bed, her hands clasped behind her head, gazing at the ceiling.

My employees. . . . Had he changed his mind? Was he intending to keep her on here? More important, did she want to stay?

She lay there debating on this, and through the indecision of her mind there emerged the picture of Adrian Stanning as he was on the day of her arrival. She saw again the little lines of pain round his mouth and the glaze darkening his eyes. Her help had most certainly been of benefit to him, for he looked much improved, and not once during the past two days had she seen him touch that arm.

Drowsiness swept over her; she yawned, hovering on the borderline of sleep. Life would be most unpleasant at times . . . nevertheless, she did hope he had changed his mind.

CHAPTER FOUR

THE sea was warm and calm, with that subtle shading of blue and green that is so characteristic of the Mediterranean.

Mary came out of the water and picked up a towel, lightly dabbing her face and legs. Dropping the towel on to the sand, she sat down, drawing her knees up under her chin and gazing pensively out to sea. It seemed incredible that it was only a month since Adrian Stanning had emphatically declared he would never employ her. For already she was firmly established, both in her job and in her home. Her office duties, so varied and interesting, were on the whole enjoyable. There were of course occasions when her employer's irritability would make life uncomfortable, but Mary had learned from the beginning that his moods were invariably influenced by the state of his arm. The obvious course was to try to relieve him as much as possible, and this she did, as much for her own comfort as from a sense of duty. Consequent on these endeavours of Mary's came Adrian's increased reliance on her, not only in her duties as secretary, but in numerous other ways. She could drive the jeep, and on occasions she would take it to the harbour or into the city to pick up something Adrian required, or to dispatch small consignments of fruit which he sent to his mother or his friends in England. At other times she would relieve him by taking the car to the airport at Nicosia to pick up a buyer or some other business acquaintance. He never thanked her; his manner was often abrupt, always impersonal, yet in many ways he showed consideration. More important to Mary was the fact of his treating her with respect. Gone was that ever-present awareness of inferiority, that expectancy of faint contempt to which she had been so long subjected.

'Mary, Mary!' Her thoughts were cut short by the appearance of two children racing along the sands towards her, one of them waving and shouting her name at the top of her voice. Mary smiled and watched them. Joy, eight, and the despair of her parents – no greater madcap had ever been born, they maintained – and Pamela, two years older and so much more mature. Tall and fair, she reminded Mary of a graceful slender *kore*, with all the aloofness and superiority of a young goddess. So different, and each so attractive in her own particular way. Joy, naturally, reached Mary first, laughing and gasping for breath.

'We're going to Salamis after lunch and taking a picnic. Mummy says would you like to come with us? Don't bring any food, and we'll call for you at about half past one.' Joy had to stop for breath. 'Will you come? – please say yes, Mary.'

'I'd love to,' Mary smiled, a surge of pleasure rising.

'Daddy said between half past one and two o'clock,' corrected Pamela in sedate tones. 'We can't say if we'll be ready by half past one.'

Her sister turned, retorting swiftly,

'It's only because you take so long to get ready – fussing with your hair and your clothes! I'm going in my shorts and sun-top. Are you going in your shorts, Mary?'

'No, I don't think so,' she smiled. 'I'll put on that blue dress that you like so much.'

'The very short one?' and when Mary nodded, 'That will do, it shows your lovely tan. Mummy says it's not fair that you brown so beautifully and she just goes red.'

'Joy, you don't repeat what Mummy says.' Pamela turned to Mary. 'Don't take any notice of her; Mummy didn't mean that she was jealous of you.'

'I'm quite sure she didn't.' Mary glanced up into the serious grey eyes and smiled. 'Don't look so troubled, Pam. I wouldn't take offence, you know that.'

Pamela's face cleared and a responsive smile flickered.

'Are you coming in with us?' she asked, with a mixture of hope and doubt as she glanced at Mary's wet costume.

'Of course she is!' Joy grabbed Mary's hand, trying to

pull her up, and when Mary resisted, 'Come on, Pam, get hold of the other one and let's drag her in!'

'If Mary doesn't want to. . . .' began Pamela, but her sister interrupted, telling her again to take hold of Mary's other hand. She stood uncertainly and Mary extended her arm, though she continued to feign resistance. The children, delighted, eventually won the tug of war and pulled Mary across the gleaming sand into the water. For another half hour or so they swam and played and then Mary said firmly that she must go. The children protested, but after learning that they, too, had come out before breakfast, she packed them off home, saying their mother would have the meal ready and waiting. They raced away and, picking up the towel, Mary stood for a moment watching them, recalling that through them she had met, and become friendly with, their parents. The Sandersons were a young and energetic couple who had recently settled in Famagusta. They had a small canning factory where the juice and segments from the citrus fruits were extracted and canned for export. They lived in a bungalow just behind the beach, and Mary often visited them, usually for about an hour in the evening when the air was cool and they could sit out on the verandah and chat.

Humming a little tune to herself, Mary strolled along the shore to the bungalow which her employer had loaned to her. He had made the suggestion a fortnight after her arrival and Mary had been in occupation just over two weeks.

'Don't you ever use it?' Mary had asked on the day Adrian had shown her over it.

'Very occasionally – when my mother and sister come or when I have friends over on a visit. We do sometimes spend a few days here, swimming and sunbathing, but we never sleep here; it's too near the house. We find it far simpler to go home than to transport all the things we should require.'

'You might need it, though,' Mary demurred, but Adrian shook his head.

'Take it for the time being. You may want to get a place of your own later, but for the present you may as well have it. It isn't good for a house to stand empty, even in a climate like this.'

'You're very kind.' Mary looked round at the furniture and carpets; all practically new and in excellent and expensive taste. 'I'll take great care of everything.'

'There's no need to be afraid of using it.' For the first time she saw the hint of a smile touch the stern dark features. 'You must treat it as a home, otherwise you're not going to be comfortable. Invite your friends, by all means.'

At that time Mary couldn't see herself having anyone to invite, but only a couple of days later she had been approached by the Sanderson children who immediately wanted to know who she was and where she lived. The next day they had come to the bungalow and Joy, with complete lack of decorum, had flung herself into a chair and made herself at home. Pamela, with more reserve, had stood in the middle of the room and had to be coaxed into sitting down. From then on they were regular visitors to the bungalow and on the day their mother had called to fetch them she had invited Mary to come along to their bungalow for supper.

Sunday was normally Mary's day for catching up on the chores which had accumulated during the week. For the island was experiencing an unusually warm April and after working through the heat of the afternoon she rarely had the energy to tackle her household jobs in the evenings. However, with an abandon which Josie would have applauded, she took a leisurely breakfast on the verandah – lingering over her book long after she had drunk her second cup of coffee – had a bath and made herself ready for the afternoon's outing. With about half an hour to spare she went on to the verandah and answered Mrs. Stanning's last letter, giving her the news of her son which she had asked for, and being able to say with truth that he was looking very well and appeared to be completely untroubled by his arm.

The Sandersons arrived at two o'clock, and Mary sat in the back seat of the car with the children.

'Have you been before?' Dorothy Sanderson, golden-haired and looking rather younger than her thirty years, turned to Mary with a dazzling smile.

'No, but I believe it's very impressive. Mr. Stanning recommended it as one of the places I should visit.'

'The ruins are Roman,' submitted Pamela, 'and from what I've heard they're very much overgrown.'

'Pam has been reading all about it; she always does when we're going anywhere. We shan't need a guide.'

'I don't think it sounds very interesting.' Joy began tinkering with the door catch and Mary pulled her hand away. 'I'd rather play hide and seek. Will you play with me, Mary?'

'No, Mary won't,' put in her father emphatically. 'She doesn't want to be bothered entertaining you on her day off.'

The journey to the ancient city took them past the citrus groves in a northerly direction through countryside blazing with colour, for masses and masses of wild flowers were still in full bloom. To the east lay the sea, now visible, now lost to view; to the west stretched the great Messaoria plain, and in the distance rose the rugged heights of the Kyrenia Mountains with their cliffs and crags, and their skylined castles topping the hills.

The whole area of Salamis lay amid a dense forest of pines and eucalyptus trees, giant cypresses and plantations of golden wattle. The place seemed forlorn and rather eerie, for no one lived there except two custodians, one of whom took the money which they had to pay to gain entry to the ruins.

They wandered about, not attempting to look at them in chronological order, for they were so scattered and, in many places, almost smothered by the vivid yellow flowers of the giant fennel. For Mary the most impressive of the ruins was the lovely Marble Forum – or what remained of it. She could imagine the rows of gleaming white pillars which had in Roman times formed the sides of the gymnasium; she could also imagine the marble statues when in the height of their immaculate glory – Apollo and Herakles; the love goddess Aphrodite and the huntress Artemis – or Diana as she was called by the Romans.

'I'm hungry,' complained Joy, bored by the spectacle of fallen pillars, crumbled statue bases and vague unreadable inscriptions. 'When are we having our tea?'

It so happened that they were all ready for a rest and they found a spot among the sandhills and unpacked their picnic basket.

Mary sat, a sandwich in one hand, a glass of orange juice in the other, watching first the children, then their parents. What a happy family they were! Dorothy, hard-working, yet always appearing fresh and ready for anything; Kevin, a wonderful father and an attentive husband; the two girls, arguing with each other at times, yet fundamentally loyal and affectionate. Mary turned away.

A strange little tremor passed through her, a tremor of apprehension as she saw her future. Since the break with Vance she had never thought of marriage, had never sought the company of men or hoped, even vaguely, that she would meet someone else. The laughter, the good-humoured banter around her became distant as she continued to dwell on the prospect of her future. She could not see herself married, with children – she *could* see loneliness and the need always to have to provide for herself.

'Mary, another sandwich?' Kevin held out the plate, smiling warmly, his dark eyes crinkling at the corners. 'Or a cake?'

'Another sandwich, please.' Mary shook off her despondency. Fate had been kind to her these past few weeks and she was grateful for this new life she was making, grateful for her friends, her home and a well-paid job – grateful for an employer who treated her with respect.

At last they began to pack up; they were the only people on the shore and Mary felt reluctant to leave. She would come again, of course, but perhaps by then the tourists in their masses would have arrived, and the place would be crowded. But for now all was peaceful and quiet. The sea, that incredible shade of turquoise, gently lapped the shore. Tall palms and sub-tropical plants – the cactus and mimosa came down from the rise and almost encroached on to the beach itself. In the far distance the sharp line of the horizon cut the two shades of blue where the sea met the edge of the sky. Mary sighed contentedly and turned to assist with the clearing up.

A month later Adrian told her his mother and Josie were coming over for a holiday. Mary was not surprised, as Mrs. Stanning had hinted at the idea once or twice in her letters. On the day of their arrival Adrian became caught up with a business associate and he told Mary to go to the airport to meet them.

'Shall I take the jeep? You'll be taking this customer to lunch?'

'Take the car; I'll hire Selim's taxi. Mother won't be comfortable in the jeep.'

The journey across the Messaoria, which in the quivering heat of the summer could be almost unbearable, was even now rather gruelling, for it was an unusually hot day for the time of the year. Occasionally, to relieve the monotony of the landscape, there appeared the Greek and Moslem villages with their flat-topped mud houses so typical of the east. Above them a slender minaret would rise, glistening in the sunlight. The contrast between the waterless Messaoria and the fertile orange groves was incredible, for the distance between the two was so comparatively short.

Mary hadn't realized with just how much anticipation she had looked forward to this visit until she saw her friends again.

'Hello – it's so good to see you!'

'Mary! – oh, how lovely and brown!' Josie's eyes danced; she was all pink and dainty and, as usual, all chatter. 'You look so well—' Her glance flicked over her. 'And you've actually gone modern. And just imagine Adrian letting you drive his car – he won't let me even touch it.'

'I don't know why,' said Mary, smiling, 'because I think you're a very careful driver.' They all got into the car, and she let the window right down. The breeze was warm, like a hair-dryer on her face.

'How good of you to offer to come and fetch us,' said Mrs. Stanning when Mary had explained why Adrian hadn't met them himself.

Mary had to smile, reflecting on her employer's attitude towards her. There had been no question of her offering. He had told her to go and taken her instant compliance for granted. She could imagine his utter astonishment if she had offered any objection, had told him, however respectfully, that driving nearly ninety miles in the blistering heat was not part of her duties as secretary. She had to own, though, that she would have offered, for the change in Adrian, the disappearance of his fatigue and the knowledge that he now suffered no discomfort from his arm gave her immense satisfaction. She had reached a stage when her desire to relieve him was so strong that she never minded how hard she worked in order to satisfy that desire. The reason for this was vague and it did not occur to her to probe more deeply into it. She was too sublimely content with her new life to dwell on why her employer's comfort and freedom from pain were so important to her.

'Tell me, dear,' said Mrs. Stanning in that familiar mild and gentle tone, 'how are you liking your job? You're very non-committal about it in your letters.' Her tone held slight puzzlement, but Mary could not explain the difficulty of discussing Adrian with his mother. She looked upon Mrs. Stanning as a friend, her attitude towards her being one of complete freedom. Naturally such freedom with Adrian was prohibited by the fact of his being her employer. Respect was demanded and because of this Mary found it impossible to write about him in any great detail.

'I'm very happy, Mrs. Stanning. I can't think I shall ever regret letting you persuade me to come.' She mused for a brief while on the real reason for Mrs. Stanning's offering her the post, reflecting on Cleone's unruffled acceptance of the situation when, out of the blue, Mrs. Stanning had calmly announced that the post was already filled and that Mary was going out to Cyprus as her son's secretary. She recalled, also, her strange fear, and the conviction that Cleone would one day cross her path again.

'I knew you'd like it here,' put in Josie, a mirror in one hand, a lip pencil in the other. 'Have you met a nice young man yet?' she added teasingly.

'I haven't noticed any around,' responded Mary, for the moment entering into her mood. 'But then I haven't had much time to look.'

'Why? – does Adrian work you too hard? You'll have to be firm; don't let him put on you the way that other old slavedriver did.' Josie applied her lipstick and brought out a powder compact. 'How is he to work for?' She turned to regard Mary with faint curiosity. 'Is he grumpy?'

'No, of course not.' Mary spoke after a small hesitation and her friend laughed.

'How loyal you are! I'm sure Adrian's a pig to you at times.'

'Josie dear, I wish you wouldn't use such language.' Mrs. Stanning leaned back placidly and gazed out of the window.

'Well, look how horrid he is to me when he's in one of his moods.'

'You're so trying, dear. You deliberately persist in ruffling him. You should practise a little more tact.'

But tact was not one of Josie's virtues, as was made clear when, after Adrian had come out to greet them, the three went into his office and Adrian closed the door behind them. Mary remained in her own office, but after a few minutes the separating door opened and Josie appeared.

'Mary, what are you doing? Come on in – we're having a chat.' Mary remained at her desk, saying nothing but giving a protesting shake of her head. 'Oh, come on in, Adrian doesn't mind – do you?' No answer. Mary began sorting some papers; Josie pushed them aside and sat on Mary's desk. 'I do believe you're scared of our Adrian.' She laughed teasingly and told Mary not to be silly.

'Josie,' said Mary, rather sternly, 'I can't come in there.'

'Why not? You're my friend——'

'And your brother's secretary. I'm here to work, not to intrude into his private life.'

This tactlessness of Josie's gave Mary the first inkling that her position could become embarrassing. A further indication occurred when, after Adrian had asked her to make some tea, Mary took in the tray. Josie began pouring the milk into the cups and Mary turned to go.

'Where's yours? Don't you want any?'

'I have mine, thank you, Josie.' The deliberate finality of her tone failed to register as her friend went on,

'What – out there all by yourself? Bring it in here and have it with us.'

Flushing, Mary stood awkwardly by the door, casting an imploring glance in Mrs. Stanning's direction. But Adrian's mother seemed intent on a critical examination of her son's features; she was obviously trying to determine whether or not he had been working too hard.

'I'm sure Miss Roberts would prefer to have her tea in her own office,' said Adrian quietly.

'But we've not seen each other for weeks! I've such a lot to tell you, Mary——'

'It can wait. Miss Roberts has work to do!'

CHAPTER FIVE

'MARY, who are these kids coming up your path?' From the verandah Josie called over her shoulder and Mary came out to join her.

'Two young friends of mine. Their parents have only recently settled here. They've bought a small canning business.' She smiled as they reached her, Joy, hot and dishevelled, Pamela, elegantly cool and composed and appearing a little uncertain on seeing a stranger at the bungalow.

Immediately the introductions were over Joy with her usual exuberance suggested they all go in for a swim.

'We left our costumes here – are they still in the drawer?' Mary nodded and, taking their acceptance of her proposal for granted, Joy went into the bungalow, beckoning her sister to follow.

'Well, they've certainly made themselves at home!' Josie looked curiously at her friend. 'Is it they who've brought you out?'

'What do you mean, brought me out?'

'You're . . . different, more free. I never quite knew what was wrong with you, but now I know your manner was constrained, as if you weren't sure of yourself. You seem to have gained confidence.'

Reflecting on this, Mary realized just how easy it was to lose confidence, to acquire a guilt complex where no guilt existed. She had at the beginning tossed her head, determined to ignore the disparagement of her friends, but very soon she had to face the fact that one's life is of necessity influenced by one's fellow men, that companionship is essential to happiness and self-esteem.

Since coming here she had lost the guilt complex, she had made friends with the Sandersons, was happy with the children, whether swimming with them or giving them tea on the verandah. No longer the dreary prospect of spending all her evenings and week-ends alone in the flat, for almost always the Sandersons took her out with them. Being new to the island they were as eager to explore it as was Mary herself.

She looked round as the children appeared in their swim suits. Joy frowned at seeing Mary still fully clothed.

'Come on! Is Josie coming too?'

'You should call her Miss Stanning.' Pamela blushed for her sister. 'She hasn't told you to call her Josie.'

'Call me Josie by all means,' she grinned, and then, impulsively, 'Yes, we're having a swim. You two go on and we'll be with you directly.' She turned to Mary. 'All right?'

'All right,' agreed Mary, and a few minutes later she was running across the sand, being tugged along by Joy who had waded out of the water to meet her.

The sea was becoming warmer, for it was now the middle of May. The children never tired of playing about; and seemed to think that Mary and Josie should have the same amount of energy.

'I'm going back,' insisted Mary when Joy tried to keep her in the water. 'Are you coming, Josie?'

'I think so. I'm dying with thirst.'

Mary made orange drinks and brought the ice from the fridge. She and Josie sat on the verandah, in the shade of the cypress trees that grew along one side of the house.

'They're nice kids, but Joy's wearing. I take it they come here often, the way they appeared to be so familiar with the place?'

'Yes; I became friendly with their parents through them. I was lucky to find friends so soon.'

A small silence, and then, curiously,

'Mum and I wondered why you didn't have friends at home – oh, please don't think we're prying, it isn't that, but you're so ... nice, and we couldn't help feeling there was some reason why you seemed reluctant to mix.'

Mary dropped a lump of ice into her glass, watching Josie and wondering whether to enlighten her. She decided against it. For one thing, much as she liked Josie,

'I'm glad.' She spoke with an unaccustomed lack of reserve, smiling at him from the door. His dark eyes flickered; Mary had the extraordinary sensation that he was seeing her for the first time.

'Are you, Miss Roberts?' A distinctly sardonic note in his voice, but one of his rare smiles appeared. 'Thank you for your concern.'

She blinked uncertainly at him, but his smile still hovered and she left the office feeling oddly happy. On the way home she found herself trying to discover a reason for this, but it continued to elude her and, baffled, she eventually dismissed it altogether from her mind.

'He told Mum he was very satisfied with you,' Josie said, and took a long drink. 'Unusual for our Adrian. He invariably takes everything for granted and spares the praise.'

Mary glanced up quickly but said nothing. Once again she felt that little access of pleasure, and once again she was quite unable to account for it.

In the distance Pamela waved as she came up from the shore, swinging her bathing cap, her fair hair glistening like gold and spreading over her bare shoulders. Her tread was graceful, her head thrown back. From this distance she seemed aloof and almost arrogant. But a smile broke as she came up, stepping between the plants that fringed the lawn's edge and spilled over in a riot of colour on to the path.

'A drink, Pam?'

'Oh ... please.' She sat down on the top step of the verandah, watching the shore where Joy was searching among the sand looking for shells. Mary fetched the drink and more ice from the fridge.

'Anything to eat – a biscuit?'

'No, thanks.' Thirsty as she was Pamela drank slowly, daintily, then put the glass on the floor beside her and gazed again to the distant figure, the lone occupant of the beach. 'Mummy said we have to be back by five and Joy won't come, so I'm going without her.' She rose to her feet, picking up the glass as she did so. 'I'll wash it,' she said, taking it with her into the house. Mary made no demur; Pamela derived satisfaction from saving people trouble. A short while later she was back on the verandah, dressed in a brief sun-suit and wearing dark glasses.

'Good-bye, I'm going now. I've hung my costume on the fence.' She ran down the steps, turned to wave, and sped on and out of sight through the trees.

'I wonder why Joy won't come.' Mary frowned as she looked along the shore. Joy glanced up and Mary beckoned her with an urgent gesture of her hand. To her amazement Joy ignored it and Mary's frown deepened. It was too far to call. 'What's the matter with the child?'

'I'll tell her as I go.' Reluctantly Josie left her comfortable chair and stood for a moment watching Joy. 'I'd better be off; Adrian wasn't very pleased yesterday when I arrived late for tea. Mum's having a lie down – oh, I told you, didn't I?'

Mary nodded.

'I expect she finds the heat troublesome?'

'She's not too bad at all; I suppose it's because she's slim, and agile. But lots of people here seem to take a siesta.'

'They do; personally I think it's such a waste of time—' Mary spread her hands indicating the panorama of blue sea lapping gently at the clear sandy shore with its outer fringe of sub-tropical vegetation. Cistus bushes sprayed the land with pink and mauve and brilliant white; the oleanders were massed with buds, promising a lavish display of colour very soon. The air held a tang of the sea mingled with the perfume from a thousand scented petals floating gently to the ground. 'I couldn't go to bed on a day like this!'

'I don't think Mum really wanted to, but Adrian insisted. He says he's lived here a long time and knows what's good for us. It's a wonder he didn't give you orders to lie down.'

'He said I could lie down, or go in the sea. I should have pleased myself in any case, for as I've said, I couldn't waste an afternoon like this by remaining indoors.'

'That's how I felt — so I scampered, quick, as soon as he mentioned that you were at home. Otherwise he'd have had me lying down.'

'Will he be resting himself, do you think?'

'He never rests! Thinks he's a sort of superman who can go on for ever.'

'But he is taking this little break, you say?'

'Mum suggested it — because we've been here several times and have never gone very far. Adrian staggered us both by agreeing to take us on this tour. I wish you were coming,' Josie added, a little spark of anger in her eyes. 'I asked Adrian what you could do if he wasn't there to give you instructions, but he said he could give you those before he went. That was how he came to mention that he was satisfied with you; he seemed quite confident that you could carry on without him for a few days.'

Reflecting on Josie's words as she watched her friend striding along the sands towards Joy, Mary reached the conclusion that there was nothing more gratifying than to be appreciated, and especially by a man like Adrian Stanning who was such a stickler for perfection.

To Mary's surprise Joy left what she was doing long before Josie reached her, and began running towards the bungalow. A word seemed to pass as the two met, but Joy didn't stop running until she came to the steps of the verandah.

'Joy, do you know what time it is? You'd better go on home; your tea will be ready.'

'I wanted to ask you something, and I couldn't when Pam was here — or that friend of yours.' She was panting; Mary brought forward a chair.

'What is it, Joy? I hope you haven't been getting into mischief,' she added with a twinkle as Joy sat down.

The short curls shook vigorously.

'Mary, what does "bankrupt" mean?'

'Where have you heard that?' Mary wanted to know, frowning.

'Daddy said it. I wasn't supposed to hear, but I was out-

68

side the window. Mummy was so upset and said we'd have to go back to England. Daddy said he shouldn't have done it without more money—What were they talking about?'

Mary found herself actually trembling at this news, but she quietly told Joy not to trouble herself about it, and most certainly she must not mention it to anyone else.

Mary had suspected from the first that the Sandersons were having a struggle, for quite often Dorothy would work long hours in the factory. But she had concluded that they were gradually building up their business and that one day everything would be much easier for them.

'Go and change now, Joy,' she said gently, 'and then go home. Mummy won't want to be kept waiting.'

'But you haven't told me what the word means. It must be something nasty, because Mummy was nearly crying.'

At a complete loss, Mary could only tell Joy again not to worry her head about it and after another small protestation she was persuaded to go home.

For the rest of the afternoon Mary felt utterly depressed. Mingled with her deep concern over her friends' misfortune was the anticipation of her own irreparable loss when they left the island. As the evening wore on she became so restless that she had to visit Kevin and Dorothy. She felt certain, somehow, that they would take her into their confidence.

To her surprise she found them much brighter than she had expected, and the thought flashed through her mind that there had been some mistake. However, after Dorothy had seen the children to bed and made coffee, which she brought outside on to the terrace, the subject of their difficulty was mentioned by Kevin.

'We thought at first that there was no way out,' he added, passing Mary the sugar. 'And I'm afraid we were both in the depths of despair, because we love the island. But suddenly I had an idea—'

'I thought of it first,' began Dorothy, and stopped self-consciously as if realizing that it didn't matter in the least whose idea it was.

'Yes, you did.' He smiled at her, dispelling her embarrassment. 'A friend of ours – a school friend of mine, in fact – wrote some time ago saying he was fed up with his work and craved for something different. He asked us to look out for a suitable job for him here. He has a little money and said he wouldn't mind investing it in something. Well, we've cabled him and are now waiting for a reply.'

'We're very optimistic,' put in Dorothy. 'Geoff is young and energetic, and we think he'd be willing to work for his keep – and some spending money, of course – until we get on our feet. Then we can settle up with him and carry on from there.'

'You mean you're taking him in as a partner?'

'That's right; but at first we shall have to take out more money than he, because of the family.'

'Geoff won't mind that, though, will he, Kevin? He's ever so reasonable—' She turned to Mary. 'You'll like him, I know. He's good-looking too; all the girls run after him.'

'Dorothy, please don't be too optimistic, dear. You're taking his acceptance for granted – and we're not sure he'll come.' Nevertheless, Kevin's tone held confidence, and as Mary strolled slowly home half an hour later she sent up a little prayer that this unknown Geoff would come out to Cyprus and rescue her friends from disaster.

It was a typical eastern night, with an enormous moon suspended in a purple sky and reflected in the dark, star-flecked waters of the Mediterranean. A welcome breeze came up from the sea to stir the palm fronds into graceful silent motion. Mary sat on the verandah steps, savouring the beauty around her.

The voices reached her first, those of Josie and her mother – and then she heard the low clipped accents of her employer. The three came into view, sauntering up the path, their figures clearly outlined in the pearl-grey radiance which possessed the magic quality of light of early dawn. Mary scrambled to her feet, surprised inquiry in the glance that flickered to embrace them all.

'Have we disturbed you, Mary dear?' Mrs. Stanning asked, gently. 'This is a purely social visit. We've seen so little of you since we came.' With that she threw her son a rather covert glance; his own eyes flicked sardonically and a faint smile touched his lips. Apparently Josie wasn't the only one who considered Adrian unreasonable in not giving Mary a holiday. She moved uncomfortably and wished they hadn't called. 'May we sit down, dear?'

'Oh . . . of course. I'm sorry.' Mary moved to one side and they came up the steps to the verandah. 'I'll fetch another chair.'

'We were just out for a stroll,' said Mrs. Stanning when they were all seated. 'The night is so beautiful, and so cool. As we were heading this way I suggested we call. You weren't going to bed?'

'Not yet. As you say, it's such a beautiful night. I was just sitting here, enjoying the peace.'

'You like the quiet, Miss Roberts?'

'I love it; it's so different from where I used to live. There seemed to be so much bustle and hurry, and everyone getting in one another's way.'

They chatted for a few minutes; to Mary's surprise she experienced no feeling of awkwardness, for her employer's formal office manner was never once in evidence. He remained cool, certainly, but he was polite and, for the most part, interested in the conversation. He seemed particularly interested in the relationship between Mary and his mother, listening intently to their conversation. Josie often interrupted with some irrelevant and frivolous remark, and although her brother cast her one or two quelling glances he was, on the whole, much more tolerant than Mary would have expected.

'Will you have some coffee?' she asked after a while, and, turning apologetically to Adrian, 'I'm sorry I haven't anything stronger.'

'I shall be quite happy with coffee, Miss Roberts. Black, if you please.'

She made coffee and several kinds of sandwiches, setting

71

them out on a small table, and using a beautifully embroidered cloth and napkins which she had bought from a Cypriot woman who was sitting on the roadside with a dozen or so others, all plying their needles and gossiping and occasionally stopping to stare with interest and curiosity at the visitors strolling by. Mary had also treated herself to a hand-painted coffee service which she had seen in an antique shop. She used this, too, taking a delight in the attractive appearance of the table. It was pleasant to entertain after being alone for so long.

'Can you see all right? Perhaps I should have laid the supper inside. The bulb's gone in this light and I can't get it out.'

'Is it stiff?' Adrian rose from his chair and reached up to the bulb.

'It's stuck, as if it's rusted in or something,' explained Mary. 'I'm afraid of it breaking in my hand.'

'It can't be rusted. . . . There, it's out. Have you another?'

Mary fetched the new bulb and he fixed it, then pressed the light switch.

'I'd rather have the moonlight,' said Josie, and her mother agreed.

'What about you, Miss Roberts – are you a romantic too?' He stood by the switch, waiting. Mary laughed a trifle self-consciously and admitted that she also preferred the moonlight. He snapped off the light and sat down, a strangely thoughtful expression on his face. Several times he looked at Mary as if anxious to make conversation with her, but his mother and Josie chatted all the time and he relaxed in his chair, abandoning the idea.

It was almost midnight when they rose to go. They might call the following evening, if they decided to take a walk, Mrs. Stanning said, but went on to tell Mary not to expect them as they would probably be busy with preparations for the holiday. Adrian, too, would be too busy to go out, she added, turning to her son.

'There will be things to see to,' he agreed. 'It isn't easy to go away at such short notice.' He turned to Mary. 'I originally intended taking three days off at the beginning of next week, but I have too many commitments.'

'Mr. Jacobs is coming on Tuesday.'

'So he is; that's another reason why I can't go. No, it will have to be this week. From Thursday, and then we can include the week-end. Will that suit you, Mother?'

'Of course – but if it's going to be too much of an inconvenience . . .?'

'Not at all. We'll be able to arrange it. It requires a little planning, though. Miss Roberts will assist me tomorrow.'

'Where are you going?' asked Mary, feeling she should show interest.

'We haven't decided, but Adrian's promised to take us through the Troodos Mountains – and I want to stay the night in a monastery, but Mother's not at all keen.'

'It sounds so austere. Who wants to sleep in a cell?'

Adrian laughed and Mary, glancing up sharply, caught her breath. How different . . . and how devastatingly attractive!

'Naturally it will be austere, but you won't be expected to sleep in a cell.'

'What's wrong with a cell, anyway?' Josie wanted to know. 'Would you mind it so much, Mary?'

'I think I'd enjoy it. At least it would be something different. Yes, it sounds rather exciting.'

Josie clapped her hands in delight.

'I knew you'd changed! I shan't ever call you staid again. There you are, Mum, even Mary finds the idea attractive.'

Feeling her employer's eyes upon her, Mary glanced up again, this time to meet a curious, penetrating gaze.

'So you're staid, are you, Miss Roberts?'

'Not now, but she used to be. Nothing in her life but a stuffy office job with a cranky old employer—'

'Josie!' Mary felt her colour rise and hoped it wasn't discernible in the misted half-light. 'That's of no interest to – to—'

'And she used to go home and sit there with her books, all by herself.' Josie paused, but only for a second. Her eyes twinkled as she went on. 'Where did you go for your holidays? Brighton? – or some such dreary resort where prim old ladies sit along the front and fall asleep?'

Despite her embarrassment and indignation Mary had to laugh. Her swift words of protest were checked by Adrian who said it was time they were going.

'Miss Roberts won't be able to get up in the morning.' A slight pause and then, 'I want you to come in earlier than usual, please – about eight if you can.'

'Eight . . .? Yes, of course, Mr. Stanning.' Mary managed successfully to hide her surprise.

'It will be cool, and we can work much better,' was all he said by way of explanation, and with that Mary had to be content.

CHAPTER SIX

ADRIAN STANNING was already at the office when Mary arrived the following morning; she looked at her watch, then at the clock, in order to reassure herself that she wasn't late.

They worked steadily until one o'clock, stopping only for a drink of iced orange which Adrian produced from a small fridge in his office. Mary became more and more puzzled, for although it was apparent that the purpose of this haste was to 'straighten up' so that her employer could go on his holiday with an easy mind, he had her doing work which could quite easily be left for another day or so.

At lunch time she took in some letters for him to sign; after placing them on the desk she turned to go, but he called her back. To her surprise he thanked her for coming early, and for her co-operation in working so hard all the morning.

'It has enabled me to clear up everything of immediate importance. I've arranged for Takis, one of the workers, to deal with any inquiries or phone calls which may come in between now and Monday. He's quite capable and has done this for me before.'

'Monday . . .?'

'My mother and sister are most concerned about you, Miss Roberts.' He paused and again one of his rare smiles appeared, although, noting the slight sardonic twist to his lips, Mary wondered what was coming next. 'I've been accused of selfishness – even heartlessness, if I remember correctly – in not allowing you a holiday while taking one myself.' Another pause. 'That is of course one of the disadvantages of employing a friend of the family.'

Mary made a flustered little gesture; she was all apology and confusion.

'I'm sorry, Mr. Stanning. Please take no notice – I

75

wouldn't expect you to extend any favours on that account.'

'That's just as well, Miss Roberts.'

The quip increased her confusion; she wondered if it were his intention that it should.

'It's – it's Josie,' she stammered. 'She doesn't understand, and seems to think—'

'My sister's clumsy thrusts I can withstand, but my mother. . . .' His slim brown fingers reached absently for a silver paper knife lying beside the blotter. 'My mother employs a much more subtle form of attack . . . which I believe you have already encountered.'

So they had discussed her. That was, she supposed, only natural.

'She told you about persuading me?' Mary's surprise at the trend of the conversation was lost in the satisfaction of knowing that her employer was now aware that the pressure had come from his mother and not, as he had so quickly assumed, from Mary herself.

'She said it was owing to the difficulty of obtaining the services of a man, but I'm of the opinion that there's more to it than that.' He eyed her searchingly and she was reminded of the interested way in which he had observed her with his mother the previous evening. 'I wonder if you are prepared to enlighten me?'

She shot him a startled glance, and at the same time a tingling of fear passed through her.

'About w-what, Mr. Stanning?'

He shrugged.

'If I knew I should hardly be questioning you.'

'There isn't anything to – to – enlighten you about.' Mary lowered her eyes, unable to meet that dark and piercing scrutiny. He shrugged again and reverted to the subject of the holiday.

'I'm told that not only must I give you these few days off, but must also invite you to accompany us on our little tour. You can of course please yourself; perhaps there are other things you would prefer to do.'

Confronted with the totally unexpected invitation, Mary

could only stare at him uncertainly. His words implied that he had been constrained into making the offer, but Mary knew better than that. On the other hand, his offer could scarcely stem from any personal desire for her company. She recalled Josie's revealing remarks last night and thought perhaps his offer had been inspired by pity. She looked at the cold dark eyes and the hard, set mouth. No, that was not the explanation, either.

It occurred to her that the reason for his invitation was not important because she couldn't possibly accept it. That it was tempting she could deny. She had promised herself an exploration of the island at the first opportunity, expecting to do it alone by coach and taxi. How much more enjoyable it would be to have the comfort and convenience of the car and the pleasant company of Josie and Mrs. Stanning, but what of her relationship with her son? Naturally it had remained until now on a strictly business footing; she could not imagine his countenancing any change. No, Mary firmly decided against acceptance. Her position would be too awkward, too embarrassing.

'Thank you for asking me,' she murmured, 'but I'd rather stay at home.'

'Certainly, Miss Roberts, you must do exactly as you wish.' His tones were crisp; Mary wondered if she had not shown enough gratitude and said quickly,

'It would be an intrusion—'

'Nothing of the kind. I shouldn't have asked you, had I thought so. My mother would be most happy if you came; she appears to be extremely fond of you – and I'm sure you're a good influence for Josie,' he added with a half smile.

Mary flushed at the compliment but reaffirmed her decision to remain at home, adding her thanks for the few days' break, which she hadn't expected and to which, she told him, she was not entitled.

'I think you are,' came the unexpected reply. 'You've worked extremely hard since coming here.' He went on to say that he was now going home and she could do the same.

77

It would give her time to prepare for the holiday, should she decide, after all, to come with them. 'Don't be afraid to come up to the house to tell us, if you do change your mind. We shall be making a very early start in the morning so as to cover as much of the island as we can in the short time available.'

In spite of her firm decision to stay at home Mary could not dismiss from her mind the pleasant picture of a holiday with her friends. It remained with her throughout the afternoon, appearing even more attractive as she dwelt on her employer's less formal attitude which made her feel that perhaps her position would not have been so difficult as she had at first imagined. Gradually she began to regret her hasty rejection of his offer, but there now seemed no remedy, as she could not bring herself to go baldly up to the house and confess she had changed her mind. Her spirits drooped as the evening wore on; even the prospect of a few days' break had lost its attraction, and in the end she almost wished she could have remained at work.

Filled with a restlessness she could not understand, she went for a walk along the shore, but the silence now seemed oppressive and she soon returned to the house. She was about to go to bed when Mrs. Stanning and Josie arrived. Mary's heart gave a little jerk, for she knew exactly why they had come.

'We've been expecting you all the evening,' Mrs. Stanning began, occupying the chair Mary had put for her. 'Adrian told us you were reluctant to come with us, but we felt sure you'd accept the invitation after you'd thought about it for a while. You don't want to stay here on your own, surely?'

'No,' she admitted, 'but as I said to Mr. Stanning, I felt it would be an intrusion.'

'How can it be,' Josie put in, 'when we all want you to come?'

All ...? Mary wondered if that were quite literally true, but of course she could not ask.

'I would like to come ... but will Mr. Stanning care for

78

the idea of my – er – tagging along? I mean, three women. . . .'

'I daresay he's not exactly thrilled at the prospect,' his mother admitted. 'But Adrian's neglected us so much on our previous visits that he feels it his duty to take us around. One more isn't going to make any difference.'

'Well . . . if you really think he won't mind.'

'If Adrian minded he wouldn't have asked you,' came the blunt response from Josie, and her mother gave a little nod of agreement. Mary made no further protest and very soon her visitors departed, warning her to be ready to start at eight o'clock the following morning.

The car arrived promptly; Adrian put Mary's suitcase in the boot and then opened the door for her.

'Aren't you sitting in the front?' Mary looked uncertainly at the empty seat, and then at Mrs. Stanning, reclining comfortably in the back with Josie.

'No, dear, I never like the front. You don't mind sitting there, do you?'

Mary shook her head and slipped into the seat. Their way took them past the Sandersons' bungalow and Mary asked, rather apologetically, if Adrian would stop for a moment so that she could tell her friend that she would be away from home for a few days.

Dorothy came to the door with her and glanced curiously at the car and the driver before asking Mary how long she would be away.

'Only until Sunday. I'll come round if we get back reasonably early.'

'Yes, do that. We'll have heard something of Geoff's plans by then, I hope. Have a good time.'

'I think I shall,' Mary smiled. 'Good-bye.'

'Don't forget to stop at the office,' Mrs. Stanning reminded Adrian as soon as they were on their way again. 'I left my handbag there yesterday,' she explained, turning to Mary. 'I don't need it, but there's money in it and a few private papers.'

Adrian pulled up on the front, then remembered he hadn't

a key.

'I have mine.' Mary opened her bag, intending to give the key to Mrs. Stanning, but Adrian said she had better go with his mother and unlock the door for her.

A late post from the previous afternoon lay on the floor and Mrs. Stanning automatically picked it up.

'Are you leaving these, dear?'

'Yes, Takis will attend to them.' She held out her hand, but Mrs. Stanning seemed oblivious of the action. She just stood there, staring at the top envelope, her face slowly losing its colour. 'Is anything wrong?'

'I didn't know Cleone and Adrian were corresponding. You didn't mention anything about letters arriving from Cheshire.'

'There haven't been any.' She wouldn't have mentioned it in any case, thought Mary. Her employer's personal mail had nothing to do with her. 'This is the first one.' She moved to look over Mrs. Stanning's shoulder. 'Are you sure it's from Mrs. Bostock?'

'Not absolutely, but this is a woman's handwriting – and then there's the postmark. It must be from Cleone.' Her voice became unsteady as she again questioned Mary about any similar letters, then gave an audible sigh of relief on being reassured that this was the first of its kind.

'Unless they've been coming to Mr. Stanning's home.' Mary added. She still held out her hand for the letters, conscious of a sudden deflation of her spirits. Mrs. Stanning passed her the rest of the mail, but retained the letter from her son's ex-fiancée.

'I shouldn't think they've been coming to the house,' she said musingly. 'If so this would have gone there, too. I wonder how she managed to get the address . . . ah, yes, she did say she'd met someone who'd known Adrian over here.' She looked straight at Mary. 'I'm keeping this,' she baldly announced, and for a moment Mary could only stare at her incredulously.

'You can't!' she exclaimed at last. 'You can't keep that letter from your son. It wouldn't be right.'

'Why not, dear?' came the calm inquiry. 'It's for his own good. If this *is* the first one, and it's ignored, then she'd be very hard-faced to try again. Don't you agree?'

'But Mr. Stanning might ignore it; he might not want to see Mrs. Bostock again.' Somehow Mary wasn't convinced that he would ignore it. The fact had to be faced that he had remained single all this time, and it seemed to Mary that he might just welcome a reunion with Cleone. In any case, Mary felt he would most certainly arrange a meeting, if only to discover whether or not he still cared. If he did still care he would obviously be quite willing to forgive, and to begin all over again. 'I must give it to him, Mrs. Stanning.' She held out her hand again, but Mrs. Stanning's face wore that determined look which Mary had seen on the occasion of Cleone's visit to The Wardens.

'I shall destroy it. I'm his mother and I intend to protect him, no matter how I do it – or what lengths I go to.'

'Please give it to me,' Mary begged in desperation. 'We must go; Mr. Stanning will wonder what we're doing all this time.' She looked round. 'Here's your bag.' Picking it up, Mary handed it to her. Mrs. Stanning calmly opened it and put the letter inside. Appalled at this action, Mary tried again.

'If he should find out – and Mrs. Bostock could write again, no matter what you say – he'd think it was I who had tampered with his mail. You must let me have it, Mrs. Stanning.'

But neither argument nor persuasion would move her. Mary finally shrugged and let the matter drop. As there was no other private letter she left the mail for Takis to deal with and they both returned to the car.

'You've been a long time, Mother.' Josie leant over to open the door. 'Couldn't you find it?'

Mrs. Stanning made no answer. Adrian opened the door for Mary and as she sat down he asked if there were any mail.

'I left it for Takis.' Mary settled back in the car and half turned to the window, avoiding her employer's glance.

'There was nothing that seemed of importance.' The tremor of fear in her voice seemed so pronounced that Mary felt sure he must notice. But after a small silence he changed the subject, much to Mary's relief.

'Where shall we make for first?' he asked as they sped smoothly along the tree-lined road towards the old city of Famagusta. 'Has anyone any ideas?' Mary left it to the others to decide, feeling she was not in a position to make any suggestions at all regarding the route they should take. Besides, her mind was still occupied with the little scene that had just taken place. To her surprise – and shame – she had to admit to being glad that her employer's thoughts would not be on the letter. Had he read it he would probably have been more interested in Cleone than the holiday. Nevertheless, for a while she felt tensed, and her heart seemed to be beating far too quickly. For she could not help dwelling on the possibility of Cleone's writing again, and of her own position should Adrian decide to inquire about the missing letter. However, as she began to listen to the suggestions being made by Josie and her mother, Mary relaxed, determined to enjoy herself, for there was something most attractive in the prospect of a few days in the company of her employer, away from the formality of the office.

'Let's go right to the end of that jutting out piece,' Josie suggested. 'I want to go all over the island, from end to end.'

'We can't go all over it in four days, dear,' her mother pointed out reasonably.

'What jutting out piece do you mean?' They were nearing the coast; the Mediterranean stretched in a bright unrippled expanse of turquoise to meet the contrasting blue of a cloudless sky. 'There are about half a dozen jutting out pieces on the island.'

'The Karpas.' Mary spoke to Adrian while half turning her head inquiringly to Josie. 'The pan handle, you mean?'

'Yes, that's right. There's a monastery at the end.'

Adrian said nothing, but continued along the road, passing Salamis and following the coast round the wide curving bay. On both sides of the road the fields were still bright with wild flowers; beyond to the east was the sea and in the other direction the distant slender and elegant mountains of the Kyrenia Range, extending for over a hundred miles along the north coast of the island, cutting off the great Messaoria Plain from the sea. Bold and rugged limestone peaks shone silver and pink, reflecting back the brilliance caught from the sun.

The road began to curve inland and the sea was left behind as they passed through a countryside of rich cultivation, dotted here and there with little Greek or Moslem villages. They stopped for a break near the village of Lythrangomi and were shown over the church of Kanakaria. Mary was thrilled by the ancient church and with the mosaics dating back to the ninth century. Adrian stood beside her listening to the guide; his mother was also absorbed in the history of the church, but Josie soon lost interest, urging them to be on their way again. Adrian cast her a darkling glance and from then on she remained silent, waiting patiently until they were all ready to go.

The peninsula began to narrow and the road cut right across the interior; the scenery changed dramatically and they were in wild and deserted country, in parts brown and parched and rocky; in others dense undergrowth clothing the low hills and knolls was relieved now and then by the white and pink of the cistus bushes blooming in great profusion. Occasionally the scent of freesias would waft through the open window of the car, fragrant and heady. Then they were on the coast again, the northern coast this time, with the peninsula becoming narrower and narrower as they sped on towards the tip and the monastery at Cape Andreas.

Mrs. Stanning had brought flasks and after she had suggested they stop for refreshment Adrian obligingly found a deserted little bay and they sat on the warm sand drinking coffee and eating the home-made biscuits which Mrs. Stanning had baked the previous day.

'Just look at that sea!' Josie exclaimed. 'What colour would you call it, Mary?'

'I don't know. . . .' Turquoise was the colour usually associated with the Mediterranean, but there was something more subtle in the blending of blues and greens on this side of the island. 'But it's heavenly,' she breathed, her eyes glowing with a strange new light in their depths.

The change in her life, from the humdrum existence of the past four years, had been so swift and dramatic that she was still dazed by the wonder of it all. It seemed incredible now that she had so easily resigned herself to the dull round of office and flat, that she had allowed her unfortunate experience to crush her for so long. It had certainly been a lucky circumstance that had brought her and Josie together.

'More coffee, Mary dear?' Mrs. Stanning held out the flask. 'Adrian, pass Mary's cup.'

As Adrian took it from her Mary was struck by his expression. His eyes met hers, flickering in faint puzzlement before they moved to rest thoughtfully on his mother's face. Mrs. Stanning re-filled Mary's cup and Adrian passed it back. He was clearly perplexed by his mother's attitude towards her, thought Mary, realizing that the older woman's manner had nothing to do with the letter. It was clearly one of gratitude, and when again she met her employer's gaze Mary felt a little catch of uneasiness – vague and indefinable, yet seeming to suggest the lurking of a danger of which she had hitherto been completely unaware. She felt a quickening of her pulse as she considered the possibility of Adrian's discovering the real reason for his mother's offering her the post. What would be his reaction should he learn that his mother had offered it merely in order to prevent him and Cleone meeting again? – and that Mary had accepted the post knowing this? And then, as if the two circumstances were in some way linked, Mary reflected on the tone in Cleone's voice when she had spoken about having seen her picture in the paper. Could her employer find out about that, too? A choking little tightness caught Mary's throat and she knew a moment's panic before, determinedly, she shook it off.

It was beyond the range of possibility that either of these facts could ever be disclosed to Adrian. Her fears were stupid and quite unnecessary.

They had finished their coffee and Mrs. Stanning had packed up the flasks and cups when she said with faint anxiety,

'Adrian dear, you're rubbing that arm. Is it troubling you?'

He looked up, surprised, yet at the same time there was a darkness in his eyes as if reflecting pain.

'Was I rubbing it? I hadn't realized.' He had not answered her question and the omission increased her anxiety.

'I didn't think about it, when we were badgering you to take us on this trip, but I do remember now that you once mentioned that too much driving caused you discomfort.' She threw a glance of apology at Mary and then went on to say that perhaps they should abandon the trip and return home at once.

'Nonsense, Mother. How you do fuss!' His tone was half impatient, half amused. He made a slight, peremptory gesture, indicating to Mary that he wanted her to pass him the picnic basket. This she did and Adrian took it and put it in the back of the car.

'Are we ready?' His mother still looked uncertain and Mary felt this anxiety as they continued, at a rather more leisurely pace, towards the extreme north-eastern tip of the island. This slackening of their speed could have been put down to the deterioration of the road – for it was now no more than a rough and boulder-strewn cart track – but Mary sensed that Adrian's arm was in fact beginning to trouble him, and she felt immeasurably relieved when at last they arrived at the monastery and church of Apostolos Andreas. The superintendent and another monk instantly appeared on the scene to greet them, shaking hands and murmuring a welcome in Greek. Adrian graciously replied and from then on acted as interpreter. He had been there before, so he also acted as their guide, taking them first of all on to the terrace.

'Down these steps,' he said and, turning to glance at his mother, 'All right?' She nodded and they followed him down the flight of steps cut in the rocks below the terrace. Then they passed through an opening in the cliff wall and entered a dim and cave-like chamber with a vaulted roof and rough stone walls. 'This is the only remaining part of the ancient monastery,' he explained, leading the way over to the well in the corner. 'As you saw, all the rest of the buildings are modern. This was one of the old chapels.'

According to legend, Adrian went on to say, St. Andrew used the well both for drinking and washing. It was supposed to contain healing properties and each year thousands of pilgrims came to be cured of their various ailments.

The atmosphere was chilly and damp; Josie shivered and said she had had enough.

'I'm not sure I want to sleep in a monastery after all,' she said as they came up once more on to the terrace.

'You don't sleep down there.' Adrian gave his sister a disparaging glance. 'In any case, we wouldn't be staying here; we've a long way to go yet.'

They went into the new church, which was built above the old chamber. Here was the sacred icon of St. Andrew, also believed to possess healing powers. A most odd assortment of silver models of various parts of the body had been put in the church by people who had been cured by the saint. There were hands and arms, legs, eyes and noses, and even hearts.

The superintendent and a lay brother had appeared, to hover about and talk now and then to Adrian.

'What are they saying?' Josie wanted to know, eyeing the votive offerings with some distaste.

'They say one must have faith, and a clear conscience,' her brother obligingly repeated. 'Otherwise he will not be cured. Many of these votive offerings are very ancient, and very hightly treasured here.'

Mary was at the back of the church, fascinated by the

row of nude figures, male and female, modelled out of wax. They stood about three to four feet high, looking rather like dolls in a shop window.

She turned as Adrian and his mother came and joined her.

'What are they?' she asked with interest, noticing that, while some were undoubtedly old, others seemed to be quite recent gifts to the church.

'Apparently they represent the souls of people who have been cured by the healing powers of the saint.'

The lay brother then showed them the sleeping quarters where guests were accommodated for the night. The rooms each had four beds and a few other items of furniture; the floor boards were bare, but everything was spotlessly clean.

'I don't mind bare boards,' Mrs. Stanning commented, 'but I do like a room to myself.' She looked up at her son. He was smiling, and a quizzical light softened the customary metallic glint in his eyes. 'Must we stay at a monastery, dear?'

'It wasn't my suggestion,' he reminded her. 'Josie and Miss Roberts were most enthusiastic over the idea.' He transferred his gaze to Mary, regarding her with that same hint of amusement. A faint fluttering of her pulse registered, but so fleetingly that it was gone even before she could begin to grasp its significance.

'I did say it would be a change,' she owned, 'but it isn't imperative that we stay the night at a monastery.' She looked across at Josie, who promptly said that they must stay at a monastery because it was the done thing.

'I wouldn't mind this at all; it was just that creepy place down below that gave me the jitters. We can stay at one, can't we, Adrian?'

'If Mother is happy about it, yes. Otherwise, no.' His tone was firm and decisive, forbidding any further discussion of the matter. He turned, thanking the lay brother for his trouble, and after placing his money gift in the box he led the way out to the car again.

'Kyrenia now, and we'll stay the night,' he decided, slipping down into the driver's seat. They passed along the same road on which they had come, occasionally meeting peasant women walking barefoot, with that easy graceful movement which characterizes the women from the Karpas.

'They're beautiful!' exclaimed Josie, returning a gay smile directed at her through the open window of the car. 'And I love their clothes.' They wore very loose-fitting trousers and open-necked shirts and were, as Josie said, unusually beautiful – much more so than the women from other parts of the island.

After stopping for lunch they had just resumed their journey to Kyrenia when Mary said, almost without realizing her impulsiveness,

'Mr. Stanning, shall I drive for a little while?'

A small silence, and then, to her surprise,

'Thank you, Miss Roberts. I'll find a suitable place to stop.'

The change over was made and Mary drove for the rest of the way. It was the first time she had driven Adrian and she couldn't help experiencing a slight nervousness, feeling sure he would be regarding her every move in silent criticism.

'I'd like to drive this car,' said Josie after a while.

'No doubt you would, but you're not going to.'

'You're mean, Adrian! I'm a very good driver, aren't I, Mary?'

'I think you are, yes,' returned Mary staunchly, and was immediately aware of the quick but faint smile that came to Adrian's lips.

'We'll stay at the Dome,' he said, changing the subject.

The Dome Hotel was built right on the sea, and had its own private bathing facilities.

'Hurry up and we'll have a swim,' Josie said as they were being shown up to their rooms. 'Are you coming in, Adrian?'

'Probably – in a little while.'

Mary's room looked over to the Kyrenia Mountains, not more than a couple of miles distant. Josie's room was next to it, and Mary had scarcely had time to unpack her night things when her friend knocked and came in. She was in a beach robe with her swim-suit underneath.

'Are you ready?' exclaimed Mary. 'I don't know how you do it!'

'I want to get into that lovely sea. Be quick – come on, I'll help you.'

'I've finished – there isn't much to unpack, but I just want to hang these dresses.' Mary hung them in the wardrobe and then, picking up her swim-suit and robe, she turned to go into the bathroom.

'I won't be long – but why don't you go and I'll join you in a few minutes?'

'I'll wait—' Josie stopped. The door was ajar and her mother came into the room, her face pale and an expression of deep anxiety in her eyes. 'Mother, is anything wrong?'

'Very wrong.' She turned. 'Mary, that letter from Cleone – I've opened it—'

'Oh . . . you haven't!'

'Certainly I have; I'd every intention of doing so. I want to know what's going on.' In spite of her uneasiness she spoke in her usual calm and unruffled manner, completely ignoring Mary's shocked expression. 'As I thought, it's the first letter she's sent to him. But she's clever, that girl. It's full of regrets and apologies – and excuses for her youth at the time. She wants to come over and see him.'

'Come here?' Mary's voice was unsteady; for a moment she forgot Mrs. Stanning's outrageous action in tampering with her son's mail. 'Do you think he'll agree to see her?'

'How can he? He doesn't know anything about the letter.'

'But she'll write again, Mrs. Stanning, she's sure to.' Mary wondered at the sudden dejection that came over her. Why should her spirits sink like this at the idea of her employer and his ex-fiancée meeting again?

'Would someone mind telling me what this is all about?' asked Josie, unable to maintain her silence any longer. 'I take it that, somehow, you two have kept one of Adrian's letters?'

'Yes, dear, we have.' Mrs. Stanning turned to Mary. 'Wasn't it lucky that we did get hold of it first—?'

'We?' Mary almost jumped. 'I didn't agree to taking it!'

'Just a figure of speech, dear,' came the mild rejoinder. 'I took it out of the post when I went to fetch my bag,' she went on to explain to Josie. 'I saw the postmark and knew it must be from Cleone. It was most fortunate that we had the opportunity of intercepting it.' She paused in thought and Mary's indignation increased at the use of the word 'we' again. Should anyone happen to hear it would seem that she, Mary, had been party to abstracting the letter. Not that anyone would be likely to hear, she had to own. But the thought did nothing to lessen her indignation for, somehow, Mrs. Stanning's coupling of their names had given her a slight feeling of guilt. 'I think,' went on Mrs. Stanning thoughtfully, 'that Adrian ought to marry someone else – and quickly. I agree with you, Mary, that Cleone will write again; she isn't going to be headed off so easily.' She sat down on the edge of the bed, a frown creasing her brow. 'Yes, he must marry someone else. . . .' A silence followed and then Josie burst out laughing. Her mother lifted her eyes and regarded her in surprise for some moments. 'What is it that you find so amusing?' she inquired in mild and even tones. 'I find the situation very serious indeed.'

'Mary's face. Oh . . . it's a picture! When you mentioned Adrian marrying she positively said "Well, don't look at me!".'

'I did no such thing—!'

'I had actually thought of Mary.' Astounded at this cool admission, Mary could only stare, bereft of speech. But fleetingly she had a mental picture of the scene on the evening when Mrs. Stanning had calmly informed Cleone that Mary was going out to Cyprus as her son's secretary. 'You like Adrian, don't you, Mary?'

'Like . . . well, yes, of course I do, but not in that sort

of way. . . .' Mary caught her breath, staggered by a sudden revelation. A flush rose to her cheeks; desperately she tried to hide her confusion. 'This conversation's ridiculous.' She glanced at Josie. 'I'll go and change – and we can have that swim—'

'Why is the conversation ridiculous?' Mrs. Stanning interrupted as Mary made for the bathroom. 'I'm sure I'd enjoy having you for a daughter—'

'And I'd love having you for a sister,' put in Josie, obviously teasing, but Mary had had enough.

'Stop it!' she flashed, and then, scarcely realizing what she said, 'I can't marry your son, Mrs. Stanning!'

'Why not, dear?' Mary gaped at her, speechless. She felt sure that, if Mrs. Stanning suddenly decided to rob a bank, and someone protested, she would look at them with that stare of mild surprise and say, quite calmly, 'Why not, dear? 'Well?' she encouraged as Mary continued to stare.

'For one thing, Adrian hasn't asked her,' submitted Josie, deciding to come to the rescue. 'Also—' she cast an apologetic glance in Mary's direction but spoke to her mother, 'I don't believe our Adrian has even noticed Mary as a woman.'

'Certainly he hasn't,' Mary agreed, grateful for Josie's intervention. 'To Mr. Stanning I'm just another employee.' What would he think, could he know of this conversation? Mary found to her surprise that she was on the verge of laughter, but she successfully controlled herself, afraid that it must surely be hysterical laughter.

'That's only because you haven't gone the right way about it, Mary. You're too aloof with my son, you don't push yourself and make him notice you.'

For a moment Mary became speechless again. Surely no doting mother of a precious son had spoken to a woman like this before!

'Push? I wouldn't know how—'

'You don't have to know, it's instinctive.'

Mary lifted a hand in a sort of pleading gesture.

'Mrs. Stanning, please stop all this nonsense. It isn't amusing by any means.'

'You're right, it isn't amusing,' Mrs. Stanning agreed with some fervour. 'And as for this being nonsense — I've never been more serious in my life. I shall be eternally grateful if you will do this for me, dear.'

'Do what?' asked Mary absently. She was recollecting that Mrs. Stanning had once before vowed to be eternally grateful — on the occasion when she had asked Mary to consider going over to Cyprus.

'What Mother means,' interposed Josie, her eyes alight with merriment, 'is that she would be happy to see you chasing our Adrian, and happier still if you managed to catch him.'

'Josie dear, you have the most crude way of putting things.'

'But that's what you meant.'

'Of course. But I myself would have found a more delicate way of explaining.' She looked up at Mary and smiled. 'You're a lovely girl, my dear—'

'Mrs. Stanning, please—'

'—and I'm sure you'd be successful, if you really gave your mind to it. You've said you like him, and he'll like you, too, when he gets to know you better. I used to think he was quite happy in his single state, but now I feel he should be married. As for you, it will give you security. I think it will be an excellent arrangement.' She spoke with that cool and quiet inflection that in itself seemed baffling and Mary began to wonder why she argued or protested. Better to adopt a firmer attitude and tell Mrs. Stanning that she considered her suggestion preposterous and give her to understand that the matter must immediately be dropped. But as she stood there looking down at Adrian's mother it gradually dawned on Mary that she was becoming intrigued, for she guessed there was more to it than appeared on the surface. After a slight hesitation she murmured curiously,

'Is it just your son's welfare you're concerned with, Mrs.

Stanning, or have you some other reason for wishing him to marry – to marry someone else?'

An appreciative glance answered her for the moment, but eventually Mrs. Stanning spoke.

'Primarily I'm concerned with Adrian's happiness—'

'I'm sure he can take care of that himself.'

'You think so? Men are really very helpless, Mary, when you get to know them. The strongest is putty in the hands of a determined woman.' She paused and although Mary smiled at this statement she didn't bother to waste time contradicting it. She had her own opinions of Adrian's strength, and they differed widely from those of his mother. 'As I was saying, I am primarily interested in my son's happiness, but I must admit I'd like to punish Cleone for the terrible way she hurt Adrian.' There was a pause and Mary recalled her own conviction that a she-devil lay beneath that mild and placid exterior. A staunch and sincere friend, but an enemy to be greatly feared, was Mary's conclusion; she remembered Mrs. Stanning's saying that her son took after her and for no reason at all a little stab of fear touched her heart. 'Nothing would give me greater satisfaction than to see Cleone suffer for what she did,' continued Mrs. Stanning, 'and she would suffer if, now that she's free to try and win him back, Adrian should marry someone else.'

Mrs. Stanning was in deadly earnest, just as she had been in deadly earnest the night she had persuaded Mary to agree to go to Cyprus. A smile came fleetingly to Mary's lips; she couldn't help saying,

'Just supposing I did agree to your suggestion, and that I succeeded, I could then find myself married to a man who loved another woman. Has this never occurred to you – or are you not concerned about my feelings?'

'So you *are* going to try?' Josie clapped her hands in delight. 'I never thought for a moment you'd fall in with Mother's suggestion—'

'No, I'm not going to try, as you call it!' Mary almost snapped, then she looked down at Mrs. Stanning again waiting for a reply to her question.

'You underrate yourself,' came the cool assertion, swiftly bringing the colour to Mary's cheeks. 'No man, being married to you, could possibly be in love with anyone else.'

CHAPTER SEVEN

ADRIAN was in the water when Mary and Josie finally went out for their swim. Mrs. Stanning, bitterly disappointed at her inability to persuade Mary to fall in with her plan, had said she was tired and would lie down for half an hour or so.

'You've upset Mother.' Josie was faintly troubled. 'I hope it doesn't spoil her holiday.' They had reached the water; it was warm and they waded in, Josie waving to her brother who lifted a hand in response.

'She shouldn't have taken the letter.' Mary felt awkward, and she was possessed with a similar feeling of guilt to that which she had experienced on first refusing to accept the post of secretary to Adrian Stanning. On that occasion she had in the end allowed herself to be persuaded, and Mary had to admit that the result had brought her a happiness and contentment which she would never have thought possible a few months earlier. But this new suggestion was absurd in the extreme. For one thing, she wouldn't know how to begin, and for another Adrian Stanning would immediately know what she was about— With a little shock Mary put a brake on her thoughts. Mrs. Stanning certainly had a most forceful way of putting her ideas over. Now, as previously, Mary found herself not only deeply impressed, but also deeply involved. And later, as she lay by the edge of the sea, looking up at the sky, she had to admit that the appearance of Cleone Bostock on the scene would greatly change her own life. She was forced to admit also that every working morning she awoke with a sense of pleasure at the idea of going to the office . . . and of seeing Adrian Stanning, that even though she thoroughly enjoyed her leisurely week-ends she was unconsciously looking forward to Monday. No use trying to deceive herself, she thought, remembering the staggering revelation that had come to her a short while ago. No need to wonder at her anxiety when her employer worked too hard, or to ask why she should make such an effort to relieve him as much as possible.

Would Cleone Bostock write again? Surely, if she were so determined she would try at least once more, recognizing the possibility of her first letter going astray. And if she did write again what would be Adrian's reaction? His mother would undoubtedly enjoy punishing her – and her son took after her. ... Would he, then, enjoy punishing her, welcome the opportunity of revenge? That he would punish anyone else who injured him, Mary felt sure, in fact, she was convinced he could actually be cruel, but whether or not he would want to hurt Cleone was debatable. His love for her had been deep ... and he had remained single all these years. Mary could not rid herself of the conviction that he would be willing to listen to Cleone, and although it might take some time for his bitterness to dissolve Mary could not see him being so stubborn as to throw away the chance of happiness. These conclusions brought with them a flood of dejection and Mary felt that if anyone's holiday was to be spoiled by the extraction of the letter, it must surely be her own.

To Mary's surprise Mrs. Stanning did not put in an appearance at tea time, and once again she felt a tinge of guilt as she sat with Josie and Adrian. Adrian himself was not unduly perturbed, saying he had been up to his mother and found her lying on the bed.

'Long motor journeys often tire her,' he informed Mary, apparently unaware of the swift glance his sister cast at her friend. 'She'll feel better for the rest.'

But Mary was troubled and immediately tea was over she went up to Mrs. Stanning's room and knocked at the door.

'It's Mary,' she said, and waited for the invitation to enter. 'You're not feeling ill, Mrs. Stanning?'

'No, dear, I'm fine.' Mrs. Stanning was sitting by the window, and she turned to smile as Mary came into the room. 'Have you had a nice swim?'

'Yes. Why didn't you come down to tea?'

'I've been resting . . . and thinking.' A distinct little catch in her voice caused Mary to frown in some surprise. With an involuntary spread of her hands she apologized for not being co-operative but went on to say that it was wrong of Mrs. Stanning to interfere in her son's life.

'And in the end he'll do exactly as he pleases,' she added emphatically, turning her head for a second as Josie entered the room. 'No one could influence Mr. Stanning's actions — I'm absolutely sure of that.'

'I suppose you're regarding me as an interfering old woman who won't admit her son's grown up and quite capable of managing his own affairs?'

Mary's only response was a little exclamation of impatience.

'Are you two still at it?' Josie appeared to be in one of her serious moods as she added, 'I've been giving Mum's idea a good deal of thought, and you know, Mary, it isn't such a bad idea at all. I feel, too, that Cleone won't give up while there's still a chance and, like Mum, I'd hate the prospect of having that one in the family. Now if you—'

'Oh, Josie, don't you start!' exclaimed Mary, for the moment throwing politeness aside. 'I should be upset too if he married Mrs.— If – what I mean is—' To her consternation the blood rushed to her face as she broke off. But neither Josie nor her mother appeared to notice, much to Mary's relief. 'Naturally, for your sakes I should feel upset,' she added in an effort at recovery, and Mrs. Stanning murmured, in her customary cool and placid tones,

'Naturally, my dear.' And then her tone took on a persuasive note as she continued, 'Perhaps you will change your mind, and agree to. . .' She gave a little shrug and tailed off.

'Agree to what, Mrs. Stanning?'

'Don't look like that,' Josie put in with a return of her normal frivolity. 'You remind me of Adrian – all grim and stern. You know very well what Mum means. Have you changed your mind about setting out to ensnare my brother?'

'Josie, really!' A pained expression crossed her mother's handsome face. 'I do deplore your lack of tact.'

Even Mary had to laugh; no matter how ludicrous the situation finesse must be employed. Josie laughed then and the tension was eased, providing an opportunity for Mary to change the subject. But even as the conversation progressed along more commonplace lines Mary was acutely aware of Mrs. Stanning's deep anxiety. At one point she complained of a headache and taking a tablet from her bag she went into the bathroom for a glass of water. Josie turned impulsively to her friend.

'Couldn't you just promise?' she begged. 'Otherwise she's never going to rest – the holiday's going to be spoiled for her. Go on, Mary, it won't hurt you to make the promise – and you can immediately forget all about it.'

'I suppose I could,' Mary said. 'But later – she'd know I hadn't kept my promise.'

'That's not important – it's the holiday that matters, making Mum happy now. Blow the future; that can take care of itself.' Josie spoke quickly, urgently, for her mother was already opening the bathroom door. 'Say you will – *please*, Mary.'

'Very well,' came the whispered resignation. It would be a relief, Mary decided, to make the wretched promise if only to escape further pressure from Mrs. Stanning.

After dinner Adrian suggested a walk; Josie instantly nodded her assent, but Mrs. Stanning said she was tired and would go to bed early. She cast a glance at Josie as she spoke and Mary could not be quite sure whether or not that glance carried a message. But Josie suddenly changed her mind about the walk, stifling a yawn and saying she too felt rather tired.

'Oh . . . aren't either of you coming?' Mary didn't realize just how disappointed she sounded until Josie laughingly remarked on it.

'What's the matter?' she added on a curious note. 'Are you afraid of going out alone with Adrian?'

Mary swallowed, and looked up at her employer, noticing the faintly sardonic twist to his lips.

'Perhaps you would rather go alone, Mr. Stanning?'

'For heaven's sake stop calling him Mr. Stanning. Can't she call you Adrian – just for now at least?'

'Josie – please!' Mary turned away to hide her confusion.

'I think, Josie,' her brother admonished in icy tones, 'that it would be a good idea if you made an effort to practise a little diplomacy. You could then speak without embarrassing your friends. One of these days you're going to say something you'll regret.' He waited, regarding her sternly, but Josie remained silent, her head lowered. This surprised Mary, for she expected a quick and pert response. Either Josie was a little afraid of her brother, or she respected him. 'If you're quite ready, Miss Roberts, we'll go. Do you need a coat?'

'It might go cool, so I should fetch it, dear,' Mrs. Stanning's words came in a rush, before Mary could reply. 'It would be a pity if you had to cut short your walk because of the cold.'

Her son shot her a curious glance, then his eyes sought Mary's, an expression of puzzlement in their depths. But Mary wasn't particularly worried by his manner; he couldn't possibly guess – as she did – that Mrs. Stanning was determined to see they were together for as long a time as possible.

They walked in the direction of the harbour. The night was mild and starlit, with a half-moon suspended, motionless, above the distant horizon. From the north-east a light wind floated in to stir the sea into tiny waves, foam-flecked and riding obliquely towards the shore. In the shelter of the harbour the white flotilla of a sailing club stood outlined against a velvet sky, the sails quivering in the wind.

'I think we'll take to the hills,' suggested Adrian, 'if that's all right with you? The breeze is rather cool.'

'Yes, I don't mind where we go.' Her usual confidence

had begun to ebb as they walked along, for she feared her employer had asked her to accompany him merely from politeness, having been placed in an uncomfortable position by the refusal of his mother and sister to come along with them. Perhaps it was owing to the fact of her mind being occupied with these thoughts that, as they turned to retrace their steps, she stumbled and, with a perfectly normal and instinctive gesture, flung out a hand and caught at his sleeve. Adrian also acted quickly with the result that Mary found herself close against him, her head on his breast. 'Oh—' She was hot with embarrassment. 'I'm sorry. . . .' To her surprise he smiled, and a few seconds elapsed before he gently put her from him.

A long silence followed the incident, a friendly silence during which Mary lost her discomfiture but found herself trembling with another emotion altogether. She still felt the roughness of tweed in her hand and the strength of an arm round her waist; still knew that smoothness of silk on her cheek and the throbbing warmth beneath. Silently she chided herself, wondering what her companion would think were it possible for him to see into her mind.

They left the shore, taking the road into the hills. Above them towered the jagged outline of the mountains, their gaunt grey limestone summits razor-edged against the dark expanse of sky. But clothing their slopes were blocks of forest, olive groves and carob trees. Other trees and shrubs sent out their heady perfumes adding a hint of mystery and magic to the night. Towering above them high on a mountain peak, the black smudge of St. Hilarion, that fairy-tale castle of the Crusaders, merged with the sky.

'Can we go to the castle tomorrow?' asked Mary. 'It's one of the places Selim advised me to visit.'

'We'll go up in the morning, yes. But you must be prepared for ruins, mainly, though some of the rooms – and the ramparts, of course – are in a fair state of preservation.'

'It's a thirteenth-century castle, isn't it? One would expect it to be in ruins.'

'Might be twelfth-cenutry. It's supposed to have been

there at the time the island was conquered by Richard Coeur de Lion.'

The conversation continued in this friendly fashion all the way up into the hills. Several times they stopped, to glance back into the town with its twinkling lights, its vast castle and little horseshoe-shaped harbour. No wonder it was so popular with the tourists, thought Mary, giving a tiny sigh of contentment. How lucky she was! She began musing again on the way fate had acted in bringing her to this most beautiful island. A famous writer, she recalled, had once said that his first choice, should he be forced to live out of England, would be the island of Delos, legendary birthplace of the sun-god Apollo, but as that island was uninhabited, and no one was allowed to stay there for more than one night, his second choice would be Cyprus, with its wonderful Mediterranean climate, its mountains and plains, its citrus groves and olive trees, its history-steeped past and its abundance of archaeological treasures. Mary spoke her thoughts aloud, almost unconsciously.

'I'm so glad I missed that plane—' She bit her lip, regretting her words on the very instant of uttering them. She glanced up and gave a gasp of surprise, for even in the half-light she could see the amused curve of Adrian Stanning's lips and the humorous glint in his eyes. Her surprise increased to astonishment when he spoke.

'No more glad than I, Miss Roberts. I must confess I sometimes wonder how I managed during those months prior to your coming here.' They were standing just off the road, up on the hillside. Carobs sprayed their perfume on to the air, and high above something swooped – an eagle or a vulture? An eagle probably, decided Mary, for Selim had said that one or two pairs nested in the vicinity of St. Hilarion. But Mary was only vaguely interested in what in normal circumstances would have brought forth eager questions for her companion to answer if he could. For the present she was concerned almost entirely with the words her employer had just uttered, uttered with a frankness she would not have expected and a warmth that was quite obviously sincere.

'It's very kind of you to say so,' she managed to return at last, rather ashamed at the triteness of her words. But even that remark was produced with difficulty, for the change in his manner had the effect of giving her an acute awareness of her newly-discovered feelings for him, and this naturally brought with it a shyness which she feared would be difficult to conceal.

'I mean it,' he said, still with that hint of amusement on his lips. 'I was most ungracious, I'm afraid, and when I now consider my attitude on that first day I wonder that you wanted to stay with me at all.' A pause and then, 'Why did you want to stay, Miss Roberts?'

She glanced up swiftly, a sudden thumping in her heart.

'I'd come all the way from England,' she replied, a little shakily. 'Obviously I didn't relish the prospect of returning so soon, of having to find another flat, and a job.'

'I see.' The sheer brevity of that seemed to convey the fact that he didn't see at all. Mary was relieved when he abruptly changed the topic, telling her something of the romantic history of the castle of St. Hilarion.

Built in medieval times on the site of a former monastery, it had known periods of siege and splendour from the adventurous times of Richard Coeur de Lion until the fifteenth century when the Venetians abandoned it for economy reasons.

'Did the kings of Cyprus ever use it as a royal palace?' Mary asked, glancing up to what seemed an inaccessible height.

'Yes, indeed. It must have been a palace of very great splendour and pageantry in Lusignan times. It's a pity something hasn't been done to preserve it.'

With the continued relaxation of Adrian's customary aloof and rather austere manner, Mary began to feel more at ease and by the time they decided to return to the hotel she found herself almost forgetting he was her employer and regarding him more as the brother of her friend. Her conversation became spontaneous and lively and on one occasion she actually put forward a little argument in defence of something Josie had done and of which her brother did not approve.

'You're very loyal, Miss Roberts,' he said with a faint smile. 'But nothing would give me greater satisfaction than to see my sister with a husband who would know how to school her.'

Mary let the subject drop, feeling there was nothing really wrong with Josie. True, she was rather extravagant and she had more boy-friends than was necessary, and Mary surmised that those were the reasons her brother thought she should be taken in hand.

The rest of the holiday was a real joy to Mary. After visiting the castle of St. Hilarion they drove into the capital, where Mrs. Stanning and Josie went shopping, while Mary and Adrian visited the museum. Then they continued their journey in brilliant sunshine through a region of orange and citron groves, of waving palms and sub-tropical vegetation. After a short stay in Lefka they turned south through a mountain pass to the hill resort of Troodos. After spending the night at Kykko, a monastery set high on the side of a mountain, they continued southwards, through regions of forest, of carob plantations and vine-clad hillsides, and then down to Paphos. Here they parked the car and went to visit what was left of the Temple of Aphrodite, to which in ancient times great processions came from all parts of the known world to pay homage to the goddess of love and beauty and to take part in the pagan festivals of worship.

'To Cyprus came laughter-loving Aphrodite, to Paphos, where rises her sacred shrine.' The words came softly, but Adrian turned to glance at Mary, who felt a hint of colour rising.

'Do you know your Greek mythology?' he inquired in some amusement.

'I must admit I've always been fascinated by it, but the trouble is I find it difficult to believe it is all only myth.'

'Mythology must be myth,' submitted Josie, looking rather blank.

'What I mean is, I never know with Greek history where mythology ends and fact begins.'

'But why should it be difficult? They're all fairy tales – we used to have them at school, didn't you?'

'Yes ... but I never thought of them as fairy tales. I thought they were true.'

'No, you couldn't have,' Adrian put in. 'You just wanted them to be true.'

Mary thought about this for a moment, her eyes vaguely wandering over the fallen columns around her.

'Yes, I did want them to be true,' she owned and, as she saw Josie's quick glance of derision, 'I still wish they were true!'

'But how could they be?' said Josie reasonably. 'All those gods were just bits of stone – idols, if you like – which the pagans worshipped.'

'Yes, I'm aware of that—' Mary broke off shrugging. 'I don't think you know what I mean. It's too difficult to explain.'

Adrian and his mother were in front, treading their way between the fallen stones and broken columns; after a while Adrian surprised Mary once again by saying, quizzically,

'Have you noticed the sea, Miss Roberts?' The wind was whipping the waves into crests of frothy white foam. 'Can't you see Venus rising, and being gently swept to the shore?' And when Mary laughed but did not answer Adrian waved a hand, embracing the hillsides around them. 'And what of Adonis? Can't you see him hunting here?'

'And meeting his beloved Aphrodite,' she added, preferring the Greek name as she entered into his mood.

'And being slain while out hunting.'

'Poor Aphrodite wept copious tears which brought forth all the beautiful anemones that grow wild on the island.'

'Not all. The red ones sprang from the blood of poor Adonis.'

Odd glances passed between Josie and her mother as this interchange continued, and Mary wondered if Adrian had noticed because, for a few minutes, he fell silent, frowning thoughtfully.

But this mood soon passed and after exploring the ruins of the temple they visited the museum and then booked in at a hotel.

From the first consciousness of her feelings Mary had found herself taking just that little bit more care with her hair, with her make-up and her dress. It was not that she thought for one moment her employer would be attracted to her, and yet, conversely, she desperately wanted him to notice her — to notice her as a woman. And as the days passed Mary sensed a deepening of the change in him, knew instinctively that her efforts were not in vain. So on the last evening, when there was a dance at the hotel, she dressed with even more care than usual, and she accepted the offer of Josie's expensive perfume which she dabbed on her wrists and her hair.

Adrian danced with her most of the time and when the air became stuffy and hot he guided her on to the balcony where they stood, silently, gazing out over the sea. At last Mary turned to thank him for the holiday, her voice edged with faint regret that it was almost at its end.

'We'll do it again,' came the unexpected assurance. 'There are still many places to see. We must use our week-ends more profitably.' There was not much expression in his tones as he said that, but Mary's heart missed several beats and she was profoundly thankful for the darkness that hid her excitement and the sudden trembling of her hands. Vainly she sought for some response, but as once again a trite remark was all she could muster she remained silent, staring up at the sky, a typical eastern sky of purple velvet, flecked with points of crystal that magnified themselves in the swelling blackness of the sea below. Was it on such a night that 'the moist breeze of Zephyr brought Aphrodite on the waves of the sea with a noise of thunder amid the soft foam'?

'What are you thinking?' asked Adrian, suddenly making her jump. 'Or are you merely waiting ... waiting for

Venus to pop up out of the sea?'

They both laughed and Mary told him unashamedly of her thoughts.

'I'm a romantic,' she confessed. 'And a dreamer.'

'So I've discovered. In fact,' he added after a slight hesitation, 'I've discovered several things about you, Mary, during the past day or two?'

Mary. . . .

'Oh,' she quivered, looking up at him with a wide but timid gaze, 'have you? What are they?'

He gave a little laugh at that and Mary almost squirmed as she imagined his saying to himself, 'How like a woman, to fish for praise'. But to her surprise his voice was soft and gentle as he said,

'Some other time, my dear. The occasion is not now but—' Before she grasped his intention he had slipped an arm around her and with the other hand her face was turned up and she felt the gentle pressure of his lips on hers. 'You don't mind?' A distinctly quizzical note in his voice, but Mary knew his eyes were serious.

'No,' she quivered, her lips trembling slightly but softly parted too, as if inviting another kiss. 'No . . . I don't mind at all. . . .'

CHAPTER EIGHT

JOSIE and her mother left Cyprus a few days after their return from the short tour of the island. Adrian drove them to the airport, but Mary went along too, and it was with extreme embarrassment that she heard Mrs. Stanning whisper, after making sure her son was well out of earshot,

'Carry on, dear, you're doing fine. I did wonder if you'd made that promise merely to pacify me, but I should have known you wouldn't do a thing like that.' Adrian had turned and she added hastily and with a sort of grim satisfaction, 'I told you – even the strongest man is mere putty in the hands of a determined woman.'

Mary moved uncomfortably, trying to hide her distress. She wanted to tell Mrs. Stanning she had it all wrong, but how could she do that without upsetting her? – without revealing that she had in fact made the promise merely to pacify her?

'You two look like a couple of conspirators.' Adrian's tone was bantering, but his dark eyes rested on Mary with an expression that she had seen before and, as on that occasion, she knew a strange and inexplicable quiver of apprehension. The feeling was soon forgotten, however, for Adrian's smile came swiftly, a rather tender smile that Mary knew by now, yet it never failed to bring the colour rising to her cheeks.

After watching the departing plane until it was a mere speck in the sky they went slowly back to the car. They drove at a leisurely pace, stopping at a little Moslem village for refreshments, then proceeding, still quite slowly, across the arid Messaoria Plain and down to Famagusta. Darkness began to descend as they reached the outskirts of the city, and a soft unfolding starlight drifted through the sky, dissolving the spreading curls of cirrus cloud which had been in evidence throughout the day.

'May I invite you to dinner?' Adrian almost stopped the car as he reached his driveway. 'Or do you prefer to go home at once?'

'I would love to have dinner with you.' The acceptance came far too quickly, she was sure – far too eagerly, and so she added, 'But I'm not dressed; I'm rather grubby after the drive.'

'I can't imagine you being grubby, as you call it,' he returned gravely. 'However, if you are, I don't mind – if you don't?'

She made no further demur and he swung the car into the drive.

'You can go and have a tidy up if you like,' he said when they were in the house. 'You know your way.'

'Thank you, I will.' She went into the bathroom and washed her face and hands, but when she came to look for her comb she realized she had left it at home. Her hair was blown by the breeze, for they had had the car windows right down and although Mary tried with her fingers to put it into some sort of order she was very conscious of its untidiness as she again joined Adrian in the sitting-room.

'I haven't a comb,' she said, with a hint of apology. 'It isn't in my bag.'

'There's one in my room; you can use that. It's on the dressing-table – I think.'

'You mean – go in your room?' Mary blinked at him uncertainly and a hint of humour touched his mouth.

'It's quite safe for you to do so, Mary.'

She blinked at him again, flushed, and hastily turned to the door.

Mary found the comb and stood before the mirror, drawing it slowly through her hair, her mind dwelling for a space on that first occasion on which she had come into Adrian Stanning's house. Her spirits had been in her feet, for she had been told quite firmly that she would not be allowed to stay in Cyprus, that under no circumstances whatever would she be given employment. And now here she was, invited to dinner. Her thoughts now dwelt on more recent events, on the change in her employer's manner while on holiday, on his kiss, and on his attitude towards her afterwards.

It had been most embarrassing, going to the office and taking up her duties as if nothing had happened – and for the first day it did seem as if the old relationship were to continue, that nothing had changed, for Adrian at once reverted to his previous austere way, and once or twice he actually snapped at her when she had done something which he considered wrong or unnecessary.

Mary replaced the comb on the dressing-table, swallowing a little lump in her throat as she recalled how his shortness had hurt her. But because she had come to understand him so well it didn't take her long to realize his frayed temper was the result of pain. Tentatively she had suggested he finish early, saying as an inducement that as his mother and sister would be leaving soon it would give them pleasure to have him at home.

'I don't suppose Josie would care either way,' he returned with a grimace. 'Are you quite sure you can manage?'

'Quite sure,' she smiled, and was rewarded by his saying on a soft and tender note,

'You're such a help to me, Mary. I don't know what I'd do without you.'

From then on his manner had remained gentle, and although she could not be fully confident of his returning her love, Mary was profoundly conscious of the optimism within her. Even so, she kept this firmly reined, for the ever-present image of Adrian's former fiancée hovered persistently at the back of her mind.

'Ah, you found it,' observed Adrian as she entered the room where he was sitting, relaxed, on the couch by the window. 'Come and sit here.' He moved the newspaper which lay at his side. 'The meal will be ready in about ten minutes or so.'

Hesitantly she moved across the room and took the seat beside him, twisting the ends of her hair with slightly trembling fingers. Adrian's arm slid along the back of the couch, then dropped on to her shoulders; with a firm and rather proprietorial gesture he took hold of her hand, putting a stop to her own gesture of nervousness.

'What are you afraid of?' he asked softly, running his thumb over her wrist in a gentle, caressing movement. 'Am I so formidable that it's a strain to sit beside me?' A hint of the quizzical in his tone and crinkly lines of humour appeared at the corners of his eyes. Mary caught her breath, though silently, as she turned to meet his gaze. How handsome he was! She liked the firmness of his mouth and jaw, liked the deep tan of his skin – and best of all she liked the way his dark eyes could soften with that look of tender humour which contrasted so sharply with his more usual severity, even harshness, of expression.

'No, of course not, Mr. Stanning. I don't know why you should think I'm afraid.'

A laugh touched his lips.

'I think it's time we dispensed with the formalities, don't you, Mary?'

She trembled at his nearness, but still raised her eyes to his, her lips parted one second, but fluttering together the next – another indication of her nervousness.

He kissed her, at the same time drawing her into his arms, holding her in a strong, possessive embrace. He seemed so confident, so . . . experienced. Responding gladly to his kisses, Mary at the same time wondered if he had had other women – and if he had kissed them in just this particular sort of way. Somehow, she didn't think he had.

Releasing her at last, he held her away from him, looking deeply into her eyes.

'You're very lovely, Mary. Has anyone ever told you that?' An odd inflection in his tone— No, there wasn't, she assured herself. Why . . . oh, why should this guilt complex overwhelm her now, just because he had asked a perfectly normal question? – the sort of question every lover asks?

'No,' she lied, and her head was lowered. 'Not really.' And then, to her profound relief, Anya came in to say the dinner was ready to be served.

After dinner they walked in the garden for a while and then Adrian announced his intention of taking Mary home.

They drove in silence, with the windows down, the scented night air cool on their faces. Reaching the bungalow, Adrian got out of the car and unlocked the door for her. He snapped on the light, bent to kiss her lightly on the cheek, then the next moment she was standing by the window, watching the lights of the car fade with the distance and finally disappear into the darkness.

The following day, Saturday, Pam and Joy came up to the bungalow before lunch, Joy as exuberant as ever, but Pam graceful and sedate and, as usual, casting her madcap sister deprecating glances when she thought no one was looking.

'Mummy says will you come to tea tomorrow, because Uncle Geoff will be here, and we're having a sort of party—'

'It isn't a real party,' Pam hurriedly corrected. 'Just a special tea, because of our guest. You will come, Mary?'

Mary hesitated, recalling that Adrian had as good as said they must begin to go out at the week-ends. She felt instinctively that he would come tomorrow and ask her to go out with him, and she felt she couldn't bear it if she had to refuse. On the other hand, the children would be disappointed if she declined their mother's invitation and Mary suspected that Dorothy would be disappointed too. Both children were looking anxiously at her and with a little sigh Mary asked what time she must come.

'Mummy says come right after lunch – if you like, that is. We'll be having tea about five.'

'I'll be along about four, then.'

Just as she had expected, Adrian arrived at the bungalow immediately after lunch, and suggested they go for a run in the car. Mary explained, telling him about the Sandersons' guest and apologizing for having to refuse his invitation. That she was disappointed she could not deny, but she wouldn't change her mind at this stage.

'Who is this guest – this young man?' Adrian wanted to know, settling himself down on a chair on the verandah and appearing to be in no hurry to leave. 'Where does he come from?'

Mary told him a little, but said nothing about her friends' financial difficulties.

'He's going to work in their factory,' she added.

'He's settling here, then?' Adrian's tone was suddenly sharp.

'Oh, yes, he's staying for a while, or so I believe.'

'And you're invited to tea so that you can meet him?'

'Yes, that's right.' She stared at him; his expression was unfathomable, but she sensed the presence of anger rising. 'I'm sorry I can't come out with you,' she said again, not troubling very much to hide her disappointment, and his dark brow cleared.

'What time are you going?

'Not until about four.'

'Then at least we can have a swim?'

'Oh, yes, I'd love that!' and then, 'Will you go home for your trunks?'

'There's a pair in the car.'

He fetched them, and the next couple of hours were spent out of doors. They swam, then dried themselves out on the beach, lying on the warm sand, and it was with undisguised reluctance that Mary said at last she would have to go in and get ready.

Adrian caught and held her hand as they strolled back to the bungalow. The garden was a blaze of glorious colour, for Mary carefully tended it, not having had a garden before. Along one side a welcome shade was provided by the cypresses, and other trees were dotted here and there, also providing shade.

Suddenly Adrian stopped and Mary found herself pushed gently against the trunk of a tall palm; Adrian's hands rested against the bark and she was imprisoned. The towel slipped from her shoulders as he bent to kiss her.

'Mary dear—'

'Mary . . . Mary!' Joy's voice floated across the lawn and a moment later she appeared from a gap in the trees. Adrian moved away and Mary picked up the towel. 'We can't wait,' Joy said, glancing up at Mary's visitor but not taking much notice of him. 'At least, Uncle Geoff can't wait – you see, we've told him all about you, and how nice you are – and he asked if you were pretty and we said yes, you were, very pretty.' She stopped then, as if it had suddenly dawned on her that she might be interrupting something.

'This is Joy – I've told you about her, and Pam,' Mary informed Adrian, taking advantage of the pause.

'Aren't you coming?' Joy asked in a much more subdued tone, at the same time casting Adrian a glance of undisguised animosity. 'You promised, Mary.'

'Yes, Joy, of course I'm coming.' Mary's glance fluttered to Adrian's face, and a tightness plucked her throat at the change in his expression. His brow had darkened and his lips were taut. Why should he look like this? 'You go back, dear. I shan't be long.'

Joy's mouth drooped.

'Can't I wait for you?'

'No, Joy,' answered Mary firmly. 'I shall be along in about half an hour or so.'

'I said I'd bring you back,' she began, again casting a glance of dislike at Adrian as if blaming him for Mary's attitude. 'You've always let me stay before.'

'I must go,' said Adrian shortly. 'I'll make use of your bathroom again if I may?' Without waiting for permission he went into the house to change. Mary stared after him, her lids pricking strangely. What had he been going to say? Whatever it was, he hadn't been pleased at being prevented from saying it. Still, thought Mary, trying to throw off her dejection, there was always tomorrow. If it really were something important he had to tell her, then he would obviously bring it up again.

The following morning Mary was late for work, and although it was the first time, she was full of apologies – and embarrassment, for the reason was simply that she had overslept.

'I can't think why I didn't wake,' she added, her face still flushed. 'It's never happened before.'

Adrian had taken in the post, and was seated at his desk examining it. He said tersely,

'Perhaps you had a late night.'

'It was rather late when I got home,' she admitted, remaining by the door, and almost willing him to glance across at her and smile.

'Late, was it? How late?' His gaze was upon her now, but there was no smile touching his mouth.

'I suppose it must have been after midnight. We were talking. . . .'

A small pause and then, in tones of ice,

'You were seen home, I take it?' His attention returned to his letters. Picking up a paper knife, he slit the envelope in his hand.

Mary's eyes widened, and her heartbeats increased with excitement. But she practised caution. Jealousy held many dangers.

'Geoff came with me – though I wouldn't have minded walking on my own. I think I would have enjoyed it; it was such a lovely night.'

Her words had the desired effect; his voice had lost its coldness when he spoke.

'I should have an early night to make up for it,' he advised, smiling. 'And don't worry about being late; there isn't a lot to do at this time of the year.' This was their slack time; they would be busy again when the oranges were harvested in November. 'Have you had any breakfast?' he added, as the thought suddenly occurred to him.

She shook her head ruefully.

'I scarcely stopped to wash,' she confessed. 'And I almost ran here.'

'Then go and make yourself some coffee while I read these. Then they can be answered.'

Within a few minutes he came out to her, an envelope

in his hand. His face seemed pale beneath the tan and a muscle throbbed visibly in his throat.

'Mary, do you happen to remember seeing a letter in this handwriting? It was supposed to have come either just before or just after we went away. But it wasn't among the letters Takis gave me. Can you recall having seen it?'

Mary had the electric kettle in her hand; she put it down on her desk with a little bang. Her legs suddenly felt like jelly and a painful trembling seized her. But she contrived to keep her voice steady as she denied having seen any letter in that handwriting.

'Do you th-think it could have got lost in – in the post?'

'It must have.' He frowned, staring at the envelope, yet not appearing to see it. His thoughts were with what he had just read, Mary concluded, for although he had heard her words he seemed oblivious to her presence. Sending up a little prayer of thankfulness for her easy escape, she at the same time frantically scanned his face, but his expression told her nothing. It was impossible to discover whether or not he was emotionally moved by the contents of Cleone's letter.

He returned to his office without another word, but later when Mary went in to attend to the mail she saw that his face wore a dark and brooding look, and there was the sort of harshness about his mouth that she had never before encountered. Again he seemed unaware of her presence, and she just stood there, waiting. What could he be thinking? Was he contemplating taking Cleone back? – making allowances for her youth at the time she had jilted him? Was he feeling ready to forgive and begin all over again?

A terrible weight settled on Mary's heart. She realized with a sense of shock that although she had at one time half believed that Adrian might forgive his former fiancée, that belief had been well and truly submerged by the change in his attitude towards herself. His undisguised affection and gentleness, the manner in which he looked at her and spoke ... and the tender way he kissed her. Cleone's vision remained, yes, but during the past few days it had receded so far into the back of her mind that it was almost forgotten.

And now it sprang to the fore, looming like some great black cloud to envelop her in misery. Her lips trembled when she spoke; she couldn't have controlled them however hard she'd tried.

'Shall – shall I see to the mail, Adrian?'

At her tone his head jerked up, and instantly his face took on an anxious look.

'What's wrong, dear? You're not worrying about that wretched letter, I hope?'

'Isn't it important?' The question came all of a rush and her voice was even more unsteady than before.

'Not in the least.'

'Oh,' she breathed, her whole world shining again, 'I'm so glad it's not important—' She stopped, sure her relief must seem out of all proportion. How she wished she could explain!

'It certainly isn't important enough to cause you any distress – and you were distressed, weren't you?' He reached out a hand and she moved across the room to slip hers into it. 'In any case,' he added, 'you couldn't in any way be blamed for its loss, so why the anxiety, you silly child?' He stood up and drew her close. The letter from Cleone lay on his desk; Mary caught one line before she determinedly withdrew her gaze. 'I know you still love me, and I'm asking your forgiveness—' After holding her close for a moment Adrian turned as the telephone bell rang. Still retaining one of her hands, he picked up the receiver. It was a business call which he ended abruptly. Then as he turned to Mary once more his eyes rested for a moment on the letter and she knew he was reading it over again. She watched his face, saw the harshness creep back to his mouth and then, crushing the scented paper with a deliberate and almost savage gesture, he tossed it into the waste-paper basket.

'Mary,' he said in tones that could scarcely be termed romantic, 'will you marry me?' But it *was* romantic the way he looked at her, gazing down into her eyes, waiting for her answer to his question.

'Oh, Adrian, I don't know what to say—' Why did she always flounder and use the prosaic when the occasion called for eloquence?

Her words produced a little laugh of tender amusement before Adrian said, his manner changing to one of mock severity,

'I advise you to say "yes", my love,' and, shakily, Mary did as she was told.

Gently she was drawn into his arms, and kissed until she gasped for breath.

'When, my dearest—?' He held her from him, and it seemed to Mary that his eyes had darkened with desire. 'It must be soon, you understand? Very soon.' His words strengthened the idea of his impatience for her . . . and yet somehow they seemed to hold a deeper significance. Throwing off an odd little feeling of dread and uncertainty, she whispered huskily, burying her cheek in his coat,

'Just whenever you like, Adrian. I don't mind how soon. . . .'

CHAPTER NINE

THEY were married in England, at the little village church, and the honeymoon was spent in a tiny stone cottage high in the mountains of Wales. This came as a complete surprise to Mary, for Adrian didn't tell her until the day before the wedding.

'We're going into Wales,' he'd said, and Mary took it for granted that they would be staying at a hotel. But Adrian had written to a friend who owned the cottage, and he had been awaiting a reply. As this friend was on holiday his answer had naturally been delayed until his return.

Adrian had hired a car, and he drove the eighty miles to their destination. Their way took them alongside Lake Bala, that lovely ribbon lake, made when the vast glaciers retreated from the mountains, leaving in their wake great scooped-out hollows that retained the melt-water.

'I hope you're prepared for primitive conditions,' said Adrian with a hint of humour, but not of apology. 'This place is right in the mountains, miles from anywhere.'

Mary laughed, not taking him seriously until they turned off the main road and began to climb. Higher and higher they went, leaving behind all signs of habitation. The road became narrower and even more precipitous, until eventually it was no more than a deeply-rutted cart track. The hedges, which no one had bothered to clip, touched the sides of the car, and Adrian had to slow down almost to a crawl for the last half mile or so, because of the mud-filled ruts in the lane. At last he turned sharply into a gateway between two high stone walls and Mary couldn't stifle the little gasp that rose to her lips when she saw what confronted her.

The cottage quite literally nestled on a tiny plateau on the mountainside, with the Welsh massif rising, rugged and gaunt, to merge with the sky. The slopes of the mountains were forested in many places but in others they were naked crags, or laden with scree. High in the distance a cwm lake glistened, and above it a much smaller lake, a mountain tarn, occupied a shallow rock basin scoured out by the mighty forces of ice and snow.

'Well?' Adrian stood beside her; his arm came about her shoulders and he drew her close against him. 'What do you think of my paradise in the clouds?'

'I think it's wonderful,' she had to admit, though she did shiver slightly as she pictured it in the winter. 'How long is it since anyone lived here? Just look at the garden!' It was completely overrun with weeds, mainly ferns and mosses. But there were some pretty shrubs which flowered in the spring, and on two sides of the garden were tall trees, pines for the most part.

'Menna and Ewan keep it as a week-end retreat,' he informed her. 'But they're not here every week-end – as you can see by the state of the garden. However,' he added on a reassuring note, 'it's not at all bad inside. Come on, we'll unload the luggage when we've explored the place.'

He found the key in a plant pot in the porch, then unlocked the studded oak door and they entered a tiny hall, to one side of which was, to Mary's great astonishment and delight, a beautifully fitted modern bathroom.

'But have they hot water? I shouldn't have thought there would be water at all, right up here!'

'Water – *and* electricity. Menna and Ewan have been doing the place up – gradually.'

'Well!' She stared in disbelief as she followed him into the living-room. 'Just imagine having electricity— Oh, Adrian, how perfectly delightful!'

Every wall of the living-room was of stone blocks. The doors were heavily studded and great oak beams supported the ceiling. Three of the walls had been lime-washed so many times that it was difficult to see the places where the great blocks joined. The fireplace occupied almost the whole of the other wall and, like the wall itself, was built of stone, rough-hewn and haphazardly put together. The mantelshelf was of slate and so was the hearth. On the mantelshelf was a miscellany of odds and ends and when Mary remarked on these Adrian informed her that they had come from many parts of the world, for Menna had been 'blessed with itchy feet' as she termed it. But on her marriage to Ewan she had neither the money nor the inclination to wander.

'She was mad on travel, but wasn't overloaded with cash, so it was always the cheapest way with Menna and instead of costly souvenirs she'd bring back a bit of rock or a sea-shell – or even a seed pod, as you can see.' Mary had picked up the giant pod, gingerly for she felt she really had no right to touch it at all. 'That, I think she said,' went on Adrian, 'was from the West Indies – Dominica. These shells were from another West Indian island and ... what have we here? – oh, yes, part of a tree trunk, petrified. She found that on a coal tip here in Wales.'

'And this?'

'That's a piece of limestone she pinched from somewhere near the Sphinx in Egypt.' He leant over her to point out some circular marks. 'Prints of a snail that lived millions of years ago.'

'But how fascinating! I'd never even thought of such things. How could she find this particular piece of stone with these marks on it?'

'She seems to be lucky; spots things no one else can see.'

There were numerous other unusual articles of interest scattered about the place, but Adrian was already leading the way into the kitchen and Mary followed. Like the bathroom, it was modern. Both had at one time been outhouses, though attached to the cottage.

The spiral staircase was of slate, each step worn in the centre by generations of people who had used it.

'I've never seen a slate staircase before.' It was so narrow and winding that Adrian sensed her nervousness and held out his hand for her to grasp.

In one bedroom everything was under dust covers, but the other room was ready for use. On the bed was a note;

Adrian picked it up, smiling humorously as he read it before handing it to Mary.

'The bed's aired, but switch on the room heater as soon as you arrive. We don't think you'll be cold! – but the blanket's plugged in just in case. The switch is under the pillow. Wish we could have met Mary, but Mum and Dad are going on holiday and we're staying at their place so as to see to Nain. There's plenty of tinned meat and fruit in the pantry should you run short – though Ewan says you won't need food! We send you our love and blessing, Menna and Ewan.'

'They sound nice.' Mary held the note in a hand that trembled slightly and she kept her head averted to hide the sudden rush of colour that had fused her cheeks.

'They're great people,' Adrian declared, taking the note and putting it on the table by the bed. And then, tilting up her face, 'You blush adorably, my Mary.' He held her against him, bending his dark head to place a tender kiss upon her quivering mouth. 'My own dearest wife ... say something to me, my love.'

'I can't,' she whispered, her eyes wide, but a little too bright. 'I'm so full, so happy.'

'I feel rather like that myself,' he owned. 'What have I done that the gods should bless me with such good fortune?'

'That must surely be the nicest thing any husband has said to his wife. I can't think of anything so eloquent to say to you, Adrian.'

'Just say you love me – that will do for the present.' And when she did not immediately oblige, 'What – disobeying your husband the very first night! Take care, for I have you in my power; that's why I brought you to this wild outlandish spot.' He waved a hand towards the towering crags. 'No one to come to your rescue if you call for help. Say you love me or take the consequences.

His banter cleared the tension that had gripped her; she laughed, then did as he had asked.

'Not a very romantic way of saying it! I hope with a little

practice you'll learn to do better,' he teased, and then, abruptly, 'No matter what Ewan says, one can't live on love alone. Come on, let's see what Mother's packed for us.'

Together they unloaded the car, Adrian carrying the suitcases upstairs and Mary taking the food to the kitchen. There was steak and sausages, mushrooms and tomatoes – everything for a mixed grill – and after finding an apron of Menna's, Mary switched on the stove and began cooking the meal.

'Hmm. . . .' Adrian appeared, his brow lifting in some amusement at seeing her over the stove. 'There's a good smell. What have we?'

'Steak and all that goes with it.'

'What else?'

'Lots and lots of good things. Your mother doesn't intend us to starve.' She turned, holding aloft a large cooking fork. 'Surely there must be some shops. What happened when people lived here all the time?'

'There are shops, yes, a few miles away.'

'A few miles! But how did they manage?'

'I wouldn't know. I expect this place was abandoned as a permanent home a long time ago.' He glanced around. 'Where's the cutlery? I'll set the table.'

During the meal Adrian told her a little about the cottage. It had been in Menna's family for three hundred years and had recently been made over to Menna by her grandmother.

'Her *nain*'s eighty-seven now and that's why she isn't ever left alone. Menna's wonderful with her, and she adores Menna.' He paused, helping himself to more cheese. 'You wouldn't think it, if you saw Nain, but she's quite well off, and some day Menna will be rich. That's why she won't be tempted to sell all this.'

'All this' was a genuine Welsh dresser and other antique furniture, including the dining-table and chairs they were using. Every dealer in the county had his eyes on the Welsh dresser, Adrian went on to say, but Menna refused to sell.

'It's been in the family too long – and Menna is very

sentimental.'

'How old is she?' asked Mary on a curious note. All the young people she had known had preferred the modern furniture to the old.

'Twenty-six. Ewan's older – thirty-four, or five.'

Glancing round the dining-space, which was really a part of the kitchen, Mary noticed more of the odd little souvenirs that Menna had collected on her travels. They took the place of more expensive ornaments.

'I'd like to meet her, some day,' Mary said, and meant it. There was a wistfulness in her voice, too, of which she was scarcely aware, but Adrian noticed it and, glancing up from his plate, he eyed her curiously. He was puzzled, she knew, by her lack of friends. She hadn't had a single one to invite to the wedding. Her rather airy declaration that she had lost touch since going out to Cyprus was regretted almost as soon as it was uttered, for it deceived no one. Out of consideration for her feelings Adrian had never questioned her, but she couldn't help wondering if he had ever discussed with his mother the odd circumstance of her friendless state. To her relief he still did not question her, but kindly changed the subject, talking about Menna and Ewan, praising the meal and finally suggesting they share the washing-up and then go out and explore their surroundings.

'How long are we staying?' she wanted to know, picking up the apron of Menna's which she had discarded after cooking the meal. Adrian turned her round as she put it on, and tied the strings for her.

'Only a week, I'm afraid—' He bent down, his cheek came against hers, warm and tender. 'But it will be a week we'll remember for always. I intend to make it so.'

The washing-up done, they went out, into a world of twilight, where the last dying shades of sunset edged the clouds with purple and fleetingly softened the hard unyielding crags. They traversed the stony path for a while, then turned off, on to a moss-strewn track which had led in bygone days to a great baronial hall, situated in the centre of the vast estate of which the cottage and its grounds had once been a part. The world of today became remote, fading into the background of medieval peace into which they seemed suddenly to be drawn. Adrian spoke his thoughts aloud.

'I suppose Menna's ancestors were the serfs and villeins we come to know when we read about life in "the good old days".'

'There was no hurry and bustle, though, I think I'd have liked to live then.'

They had reached a particularly narrow section of track and Mary's clasp on her husband's hand unconsciously tightened.

'No.' He shook his head. 'You wouldn't have been safe at all.'

'Not safe?' She blinked at him in puzzlement.

'The great lord would have spotted you – bathing in the stream, probably – and he'd have said to himself, I must have that lovely nymph, and the next thing you knew you'd have been ordered up to the hall, to become my lord's—' He coughed discreetly, and then laughed. 'You wouldn't have liked that at all . . . or would you?'

If Adrian hoped to produce embarrassment he was disappointed. No blush appeared. On the contrary Mary surprised herself by entering gaily into his mood as she said, with a deliberate attempt at coquetry,

'I should probably have liked it immensely . . . yes, I'm sure I should.'

'Shameless wench!' He stopped as the track widened, and glowered down at her. 'What an admission to make to your husband! For that, madam, you will be well and truly chastised!'

'You haven't yet heard all,' she laughed, and added, 'You, of course, would have to be "my lord".'

'Ah . . . that's different. . . .' They talked on in the same vein for a while, strolling hand in hand, storing memories as lovers do, treasures rarer than the finest gold. Falling darkness allowed the stars to appear, but there was no moon and Adrian said they had better turn back, for the track was becoming steeper and more treacherous as they went along.

The floating dew gradually spun a shroud of lace, clothing the mountain peaks, and swirling in gossamer folds to drape, much more revealingly, the lower shadowed slopes.

But the cottage itself was bathed in starlight, for the dew had not yet risen on this side of the mountain. The tiny windows caught the light, and shone beneath the overhanging eaves. The studded oak door, which Adrian had not troubled to lock, had swung on its hinges and now stood invitingly open.

Mary stopped by the porch, and looked up, her eyes wide, and revealing all her love.

'Thank you for bringing me to this heavenly place,' she said simply, and without conscious effort it suddenly came to her that this could have been Cleone standing here, had Adrian been willing to forgive. But he hadn't been willing to forgive, because his love had died. No grounds whatever for his mother's deep anxiety, no necessity for that ridiculous promise. Mary had to smile at the recollection of that, for although she had made the promise she hadn't the faintest idea of how to set about 'chasing' Adrian, as his sister had so crudely put it. In any case, there wouldn't have been any need, for Adrian's love had developed quite naturally, in the way that all love should.

Her thoughts were interrupted by the pressure of his fingers and she glanced up again, to see the depth of tenderness in his eyes . . . and something else.

'Thank you for coming,' he returned, just as simply, and kissed her.

Hand in hand they entered the cottage. The door swung to behind them and the latch dropped firmly into place.

Mary stood by the bedroom window, gazing dreamily out to the distant peaks of the great Welsh massif. Dawn had long since brushed their ragged points with glorious gold and crimson, and now the sky was a canopy of pearl and rose, spreading its weapon of light to vanquish the last of the mist. Nearer to, the rays reflected back the light from the naked mountain sides, and Mary turned, for the fierceness of the light was hurtful to her eyes.

Adrian still slept; Mary's eyes darkened with tenderness and on impulse she moved over to the bed and bent to kiss her husband's lips. He opened his eyes, sleepily.

'What more could a man wish for than to be awakened from his dreams by the kiss of a beautiful woman? What, are you up already?'

'Darling, you've said that the wrong way round – er – back to front.'

'Why so?' He half sat up, leant on one elbow and studied her. She hadn't troubled to use a negligée; her nightdress was ridiculously short.

'Well. . . .' She puckered her brow in an effort to sort out his words. 'You should have asked me if I was up first—'

'It's obvious you're up first. You always are.'

'You know very well what I mean,' she laughed. 'Your second question should have come first.'

'Not at all.'

'Why not?'

'Because I thought you were here beside me when you kissed me.' He grinned at her, and her heart skipped a beat or two. How young he seemed, and how handsome he was! 'I dreamt your kiss was an invitation,' he added ruefully. 'Alas for dreams!'

'Idiot!' Mary changed the subject. 'It's a glorious morning – and our last-but-one.' She turned to the window again, pulling the curtain over slightly in order to shield her eyes from the sun. 'Get up, darling, and let's make the most of it.' A sadness crept into her voice and almost immediately she felt her husband's hands on her arms; she leant back against him and rested her head on his breast.

'This is only the beginning, my Mary,' he told her in tones of gentle reassurance. His lips touched her hair and stayed there for a while. 'A lovely memory for always . . . but only the beginning.'

'But it will never be quite like this again.'

'Nothing is ever quite the same as what went before. But you and I shall always feel like this; nothing can change our love – nothing will ever come between us.'

'Nothing?' Her voice faltered, even to her own surprise.

'Sweetheart . . . what's wrong?' He turned her round and she saw that he was frowning.

'I'm stupid, Adrian. I – oh, I can't tell you; it's too silly.'

'Tell me.'

'I feel afraid . . . somehow.' She glanced into his eyes, a frown touching her own face now. 'Why should I feel like this?' Her tone pleaded for an explanation, but she went on, scarcely conscious of what she said, 'Is it because men change?'

'Men?'

'They're not as understanding as women – they can be hard, if things go wrong—'

'And what can go wrong?'

'I don't know. The feeling's just this minute come on – and I know it's ridiculous, but— If only men were made like women, then—'

'—what a dull life we all should lead,' he finished, his eyes kindling with laughter as she shot him a glance of indignation.

'Adrian, please be serious.'

'I absolutely refuse to be serious about such stupid notions. I expect this sort of reaction is normal – probably every woman experiences it. Pre-wedding nerves, the strain of the honeymoon, overspent emotions. . . . No, darling, I'm just not going to take the slightest notice of your silly imaginings.'

'I'm sorry. . . .' She snuggled close. 'You're right, they are silly imaginings.' How could anything go wrong when she felt safe like this? Adrian was right, it *was* a case of nerves and strain and overspent emotions.

He turned her round again and they both stood looking out upon the golden scene of mountain splendour.

'Why do you think I chose this place?' he murmured, his lips against her hair again. 'Because I love the mountains. They symbolize all that one's ideals should be – high and strong and enduring. And I felt they'd be a symbol of our love too – strong and enduring. Haven't we already laid the foundations of a perfect marriage? Nothing can ever shake them, Mary; have no fear of that.' He spoke with firmness and confidence; any lingering vestige of doubt was swept away and Mary edged round in his arms and smiled happily up at him. His eyes remained serious for a moment longer and then his mood changed. 'You're right, it is a glorious morning. Come, I'll toss you for the bathroom.'

'No, it's my turn. You had it first yesterday.'

'And you, shameless brat, threatened to walk in on me if I didn't hurry.'

'I wouldn't have, though,' she owned, blushing. 'But you do take a long time, Adrian.'

'Thank goodness we have two bathrooms at home.' He reached for her negligée, holding it out while she slipped into it. 'Off you go, then. I'll sort out something for breakfast. How are we doing? – have we come to the end of our provisions?'

'There's everything. Grapefruit, eggs and ham. The bread's a bit stale, though.'

'A bit stale! It was like iron yesterday, so I don't know what it'll be like now.'

'We'll have to toast it,' then she added, impishly, 'Watch it carefully, darling; it easily burns when it's dry.'

'You——! Look here, don't let this fool you, my girl. When we get home I'll expect to be waited on hand and foot.' But Mary was already on her way downstairs, humming a little tune to herself.

They spent the day out of doors, tramping through the hills. Mary prepared a packed meal, but they took nothing to drink, for neither was anxious to carry the flask. So they drank from a cool mountain stream, sitting on the bank to eat their snack lunch. Then they tramped again and arrived back at the cottage ravenously hungry.

The meal this time came out of tins, but Mrs. Stanning had chosen the food with care and everything they had was delicious. They took their coffee into the living-room, where Adrian had lighted a fire, starting it with coal and then backing it up with pine logs which he had found in a shed outside. They burned brightly, filling the air with their heady scent and providing a soft illumination, enough for their needs.

Sitting on the rug, still in her jeans and sweater, Mary leant back against the chair and gazed pensively into the fire.

'This time tomorrow,' she murmured at length, 'we'll be in Cyprus.'

'We'll be home,' Adrian, relaxing contentedly in the big armchair, smiled lovingly down at her. 'I'm beginning to wonder whether I should have brought you here. You're so sad at leaving.'

'Not sad ... but I've been so blissfully happy—' She moved, resting her head against his knee; his hand came down on to her shoulder. 'Naturally I feel regret. You must do too?'

'That goes without saying, but we've a wonderful memory to take with us – and there's no reason why we shouldn't spend another holiday here some time.'

'Oh, can we? I never thought of that.' The prospect took away the little weight that had settled upon her, lightening her dejection at the thought of leaving.

'Certainly we can – and will, if it means so much to you. We'll have a second honeymoon. Will that suit you?' A quizzical, teasing note in his voice, but something else in his tone convinced her that he too would look forward to coming back. She didn't answer his question, but asked one herself instead.

'Adrian, do you believe in atmospheres – in houses, I mean?'

He did not speak for a moment, but sat gazing into the fire, his hand gently caressing her hair.

'Some day I hope you'll meet Nain. I think she's responsible for the atmosphere here. She seems to throw off love – you can't escape it.' Mary turned her head sharply, realizing for the first time just how little she knew her husband. She recalled the photograph on his mother's sideboard, and her own mental image of his character. Hard, she had branded him, and unfeeling; a man to scoff at sentimentality in any form whatever. 'Menna, too, is a rather wonderful person, very like her grandmother.' He turned a tender glance upon his wife, and Mary caught her breath as happiness surged up within her. Would she ever cease to be thrilled by that particular manifestation of his love?

'And now,' she murmured, reaching up to cover his hand, 'you and I have added more love to the atmosphere.' She spoke solemnly, though her voice reflected all her happiness. 'I'm so grateful to you for bringing me here. When you said we were coming into Wales I pictured a hotel, at a crowded seaside resort—'

'With sniggering room-maids and the usual amused and covert glances from our fellow guests?' He shook his head emphatically. 'That was not for us, Mary. Besides, I wanted you to myself. Do you realize we haven't seen another human being for almost a week?'

'And I haven't missed them in the least.'

'I should hope not,' in tones of mock indignation. 'I should be a poor sort of bridegroom if you had!'

By eight o'clock the following morning they were on their way, driving through the mountains in a thick haze of purple mist. It clung to Bala and hovered in the valleys, persisting throughout the first half of the journey.

'It's upset my calculations,' Adrian said with some anxiety when at last he was able to increase his speed. 'We'll not have to waste much time at Mother's or we'll miss the plane.'

It had been arranged that the hired car should be left at The Wardens, to be collected later. They would then drive to the airport in Josie's car. As it was necessary for

Josie to accompany them, in order to bring back the car, Mrs. Stanning had said she might as well go too, and see them off.

'There isn't much to do,' Mary said reassuringly. 'We've only to pick up the clothes we left behind.' These were what she and Adrian had worn before the wedding, and Mary surmised that they would be all ready and packed in a suitcase.

'And transfer this luggage into Josie's car.'

'Oh, yes, I'd forgotten that.'

'We haven't a great deal of time, Mother,' Adrian said immediately they arrived. He glanced at the suitcase by the door in the hall. 'Is everything in there?'

'No, dear. Mary's things are upstairs – I was just going to bring the case down.' She paused uncertainly. 'It's the leather one—'

'Too much weight. Can't Mary's things go in there?'

'That's quite full, Adrian.'

'Perhaps I don't need them,' Mary put in, her brow furrowing as she tried to remember what she had left behind. 'Shall I go up and see? If there are one or two things I need they might go in the other case – the one I have in the car.'

'Yes, do that, and be as quick as you can.' His voice was abrupt; Mary knew he was anxious, for if they didn't catch the plane he would miss an important appointment with one of his most valued customers. 'Leave as much as you can; Mother will send it on later. I'll go and put the other luggage in Josie's car.' He glanced round. 'Where *is* Josie?'

'On the telephone – talking to one of her boy-friends. She'll be finished directly.' She hesitated. 'There's a meal on, Adrian, it's quite ready—' But Adrian was shaking his head. He glanced apologetically at Mary, who was already making for the stairs. 'We can eat on the plane. All right?'

'Of course.'

She expected to find the suitcase in the room she usually occupied; when it wasn't there Mary called to Mrs.

Stanning. Unable to make herself heard, she at last went downstairs again, finding her mother-in-law in the kitchen, hastily making a cup of tea.

'Oh, it's in Adrian's room,' she apologized when Mary said she couldn't find the suitcase. 'On the bed, dear.' Mary sped away again. She knew which was Adrian's old room, though she had never been in it. It was very similar to the one she had used, having the same view, but it was slightly larger and off it was what appeared to be a small dressing-room, though Mary couldn't be sure, for the door was almost closed. It was a beautifully furnished room, with thick carpet on the floor, matching that on the hall and stairs.

The suitcase was on the bed, but even before Mary had opened it, she turned again, smiling as Mrs. Stanning came into the room.

'You shouldn't have bothered coming up,' she said. 'I can manage.'

'I just wanted to thank you for what you've done, dear. I said I'd be eternally grateful to you, and I shall.' Mary's face clouded with distress and she opened her mouth to speak, but Mrs. Stanning continued, appearing not to notice her discomfiture, 'You seem happy enough, Mary.'

'I am happy, perfectly happy.'

A slow, triumphant smile spread over Mrs. Stanning's handsome face; she seemed to be gloating inwardly.

'I often think of Cleone Bostock's confidence that night she came to The Wardens, remember, Mary? But we certainly scotched her little scheme, you and I. We've managed my son's life very well between us, don't you think?' Mary was staggered into speechlessness. Mrs. Stanning seemed to have forgotten she was speaking to her son's wife. True, she didn't know the truth, that Mary had married her son for love, but even so she should have tried to practise a little tact. 'Aren't you glad, dear,' she went on in her usual calm unruffled tones, 'that you agreed to fall in with my plan?– glad you accepted the post of secretary to Adrian? Look how well set up you are now – secure for life. And aren't you glad we kept that letter? Just think, dear, if Adrian had got hold of it—'

'Cleone sent another one.' Mary hadn't meant to say that; she spoke urgently, seizing on anything that would put a stop to these distressing things her mother-in-law was saying.

'Another . . .?' For the first time Mrs. Stanning seemed put out, though not to any marked degree. 'Did you manage to get hold of that one too?'

A tiny sigh of exasperation escaped Mary at the way Adrian's mother persistently coupled their names over the matter of the stolen letter. But there was nothing to be gained by protesting; in any case, there was no time to do so. Adrian would be wondering what was keeping her. Mrs. Stanning was staring at her, waiting for an answer.

'Adrian had already taken in the post when I arrived at the office.' Mary tried to end the subject there, by deliberately turning away and unfastening the suitcase.

'Oh . . . so you weren't able to intercept it.' She paused, frowning slightly; Mary cast her an angry glance and was about to say she wouldn't have dreamed of tampering with Adrian's mail, but her mother-in-law spoke again. 'How very unfortunate, Mary. Did Cleone mention that first letter? – I mean, did Adrian inquire about it?'

'Yes.' Mary's tone was curt, but her hands were trembling as she took out a dress from the case. In fact, her whole body began to tremble at the memory of that dreadful few minutes when she had been forced to lie to her employer.

'And obviously you didn't give yourself away. Clever girl! How did you manage to fob him off—?' She was interrupted by the entrance of her daughter. Josie literally bounded into the room and flung her arms around Mary's waist.

'I heard you two talking. Oh, you look so smart! And happy! Marriage agrees with you. And just to think,' she went on, her voice dropping to a roguish whisper, 'you didn't want to do any chasing, said you wouldn't know how; and you were so indignant with Mum for suggesting it!' She laughed and went on teasingly, resuming her normal voice, 'I think you're a dark horse, Mary. I think you must have had practice in ensnaring unsuspecting males before you set to work on our Adrian!'

'Josie, please ...?' Though hot with embarrassment and indignation Mary gave a helpless little shrug. What was the use? And what good would argument do? Some day she would make a determined effort to enlighten them both, to impress the truth upon them, but there was no time now.

'I must sort these out,' she said, and Mrs. Stanning nodded and moved away.

'Of course, dear. Come, Josie, and help me pour the tea. They must at least have a drink before they start on such a long journey.'

With a deep sigh of relief Mary returned once more to her task. All these would have gone in her other suitcase, but she'd done some shopping in England – bought things for her trousseau – so now she had this surplus. Quickly deciding she could do without all that was in the case, she pushed everything back and closed the lid, snapping on the fastener.

And then, straightening up, she blinked at her husband, standing by the door of the dressing-room.

'Adrian ...?' She spoke his name softly, in tones of faint surprise. 'I didn't hear you come in. I've decided not to take—' The blood slowly drained from her face as several things registered. The door to the dressing-room was wide open. In his hand Adrian held a box, and Mary remembered his saying he must bring back some colour slides; he'd wanted to show them to her. He must have come up when she was in the kitchen with his mother. He'd been in there all the time ... heard everything. And yet she said, clinging frantically to the hope of some miracle,

'How – how long have y-you. ...' She could not go on; her voice faltered because of the fear in her throat.

'Long enough.' His tone had the hardness of steel, but he seemed dazed. Little streaks of white had broken through the deep tan of his face, and these were accentuated at the corners of his mouth. His mouth itself was tight, drawn back in a thin and almost cruel line. But his eyes. . . . Mingling with the shades of harshness that had suddenly appeared was a terrible, unseeing glaze of bitterness and disillusionment. Mary flinched at the pain she found there; never did she want to see that expression again. Her mouth was parched, but she managed to speak, at the same time recalling one by one every single thing that had just been said in his hearing.

'Adrian, don't look like that— You mustn't be hurt. What you heard just now – those things – they weren't true—' Oh, heavens, she'd put that all wrong. No wonder his eyes had moved, to stare at her uncomprehendingly. She had allowed Mrs. Stanning to have her say, made no protest whatsoever, either then or when Josie came in to add her contribution. And she was telling Adrian those things weren't true! 'It sounded dreadful, I admit,' she went on, scarcely knowing what she said. 'But if I try to explain—'

'Are you ready?' The icy contempt in his voice made her want to cry out to him, plead with him to listen. Unsteadily she went closer, aching to slip into his arms. With a deliberate movement he stepped aside. Mary's eyes filled.

'Yes – I'm r-ready.'

'Then we'd better be making a move.' He crossed the room, then turned at the door. 'Have you anything else to put in the car?'

Mary just shook her head dumbly, and followed him from the room.

CHAPTER TEN

'HAVEN'T we already laid the foundations of a perfect marriage? Nothing can ever shake them, Mary; have no fear of that.'

Her husband's confident and reassuring words came to Mary as she sat at her desk in the outer office, her fingers lying idle on the keys of her typewriter. Nothing can ever shake them. . . . Tears filled her eyes, released at last from the agony clouding her mind. She put her head in her hands, and her lips moved convulsively. 'God help me. . . .'

Two weeks had passed since the end of that blissful honeymoon, two terrible weeks of silence – or near silence. Adrian spoke when it was necessary, mainly in the office; rarely at home. Several times Mary had endeavoured to break that silence, persevering with all the contrition and humility she knew, to make him listen. And yet even as the words of pleading left her lips she wondered what she would say, should he decide to give her the opportunity of clearing herself.

How could she sound sincere when in fact she *had* come out to Cyprus at his mother's instigation? That was one thing she could never deny. Then what of the letter? Could she throw the entire blame upon his mother? Looking back now Mary felt astounded that she had allowed Mrs. Stanning to keep that letter. Had she made a determined stand Adrian's mother would have been forced to give it up. She could have threatened to tell her son of the letter's existence; she could more simply have snatched it out of Mrs. Stanning's hand. But she did neither.

It was always easy, though, to chide oneself after the event, and say what should have been done. In this Mary felt she was no different from anyone else. Mrs. Stanning's action had come as a shock and Mary knew now that she hadn't really had time to think; in fairness to herself she found some small excuse for not doing what she had known to be right. Adrian, however, would certainly find no excuse for her conduct.

As for Josie's unfortunate remarks about ensnaring unsuspecting males – well, she could at least deny that. Adrian himself must know those remarks didn't apply.

She glanced up as he came out of his office.

'I'm going to the airport to pick up a friend,' he informed her coldly. 'Please leave the office early and help Anya prepare a room for her.'

'Her?' Mary stared at him. Not a muscle of his face moved as he replied,

'My former fiancée. You've already met, I believe.'

Mary stared in disbelief. She had known all along that he was making a concentrated effort to punish her, because she had hurt him so terribly, but she had never dreamed he would go to these lengths. How long had he and Cleone been corresponding? she wondered. Adrian must after all have answered that letter which he'd so savagely crushed a moment before he had asked her, Mary, to marry him. And they must have corresponded since.

'You can't do this to me.' She was humbly pleading, conscious as always of her own guilt, and yet still not doubting for one moment that he loved her. 'If you do you'll come to regret it – some day – when things are once more right between us.'

'Right?' That terrible bitterness again, but his face wore a harsh and merciless expression, too. 'Will things ever be right between us?'

'Yes—' Her answer came swiftly, born of fear. 'I'm sure of that – very sure.' But she wasn't sure. As she searched his face, examining those harsh lines which now marred his handsome features, she became even more afraid. Should Adrian continue to adopt this attitude of inflexibility, should he never reach the depth of understanding where her weak, unconvincing explanation could make an impression, then happiness was lost for ever to them both. The possibility terrified her. 'They must come right,' she went on, desperately. 'We can't go through life like this – so far apart!'

'I don't intend we shall go through life like this,' he told her on a cryptic note. 'No, that, as you say, would not be possible.'

What did he mean? Her lashes fluttered as he continued to stare at her. Was he intending to separate? Somehow she did not think that even in the midst of such bitterness and disillusionment he would contemplate a break like that.

She stood up; Adrian was now by the door, preparing to leave.

'Why is she coming? Have you invited her?'

'She is at liberty to come if she wishes,' he said evasively.

'Have you invited her?' Mary repeated when he ignored her question. He glanced at his watch, turned, and would have left the office had she not said quickly, 'You shouldn't bring her to our house, Adrian. It's wrong – it's going to make things worse between us.' Why, she wondered, would he not answer her question? Surely it could only mean that Adrian had not invited Cleone. How, then, did she come to be here?

He paused for a moment; clearly he did not want to speak to her. Nevertheless he did speak at length, and there was a depth of misery beneath the stiff and frigid tones.

'Things will never be right between us. If we both resign ourselves to that then life might eventually become bearable.'

She extended her arms in an imploring, yet half helpless gesture.

'You're so hurt – but how do you think I feel, knowing as I do that I'm the one who's hurt you? No, Adrian, don't go,' she pleaded urgently as he turned as if to leave her. 'Listen, just for one moment. I would never hurt you intentionally, because I love you—'

'What?' he interrupted harshly. 'Don't stand there trying to convince me you married me for love!'

'I did, no matter what you think.' She stopped and averted her head as a soft flush touched her cheeks. 'Those – those times at the cottage – those nights. ... You must know I love you.'

At that he came back into the room, his eyes roving over her with a sudden kindling of desire.

'Superb acting—' Before she realized it he had taken her in his arms and kissed her, but not with the tenderness and love he had shown at the cottage. Then he almost thrust her from him, though he still retained her arms in a hard and vicious grip. 'Yes, Mary, superb acting ... which may cost you dear.' He released her, but she still felt the hurtful pressure of his fingers. 'Surpassing even your acting over the letter. The way you looked me straight in the eye and told me you'd never seen it— Fobbed me off, I think was the way my mother described it.' His eyes darkened and Mary knew his pride had suffered as never before. She opened her mouth to make some sort of protest, then closed it again. For a fortnight Adrian had kept quiet about what he'd heard, had bottled it up inside, not knowing the whole story. And now the terrible, nerve-racking silence was being broken at last. It must clear the air, if only in some small way, and so she just stood there, accepting all he flung at her as he related, and bitterly dwelt upon, the various things he had heard on that fateful last day of their honeymoon. He didn't often give Mary the chance to speak, but now and then he would make her fill in a gap, until in the end he had forced the whole series of events from her. Taking advantage of these occasions when he was willing to listen, Mary tried desperately to phrase her explanations so that her own part in the plot would appear less culpable, while ensuring that no excessive blame was placed upon his mother. But the heavy weight of despair soon settled upon her again as she watched his expression. The time was not right; Adrian was in no mood even to view her conduct dispassionately, much less offer her forgiveness. His lips compressed even more tightly when Mary told him about Cleone's visit to The Wardens, and although it was clear that this increased anger resulted from his mother's – and Mary's own – interference in his affairs, she knew for sure that for the most part it reflected his contempt for his former fiancée. This conviction should have heartened Mary, for it was clear that, hurt and angry as he was, her husband intended bringing Cleone here merely as an act of revenge but, strangely, she was not heartened, for she suddenly recalled the smouldering look of hatred in Cleone's eyes, and her own strange sensation of fear as she became convinced that she and Cleone would one day meet again.

Adrian had paused; Mary saw him glance again at his watch.

'Please – *please* don't bring Mrs. Bostock to our house. I know you don't think it now – because you want to hurt me and this is your way – but you *will* be sorry . . . because you love me—'

'Love!' A harsh laugh broke from his lips. 'I loathe you!'

'No – oh, *no*, don't say such things,' she cried in sudden anguish. 'You can't mean it, not after what you said to me at the cottage. You said our love was strong, enduring, that nothing could ever come between us. . . .' Mary's voice sank to a whisper, and she lowered her eyes, for the bitterness that crossed his face was more than she could bear.

'And how you must have laughed, laughed at my unmanly sentimentality—'

'It wasn't unmanly, you couldn't be—'

'—and at my prattle about ideals. Who cares about ideals these days? But I haven't any now; you've very effectively shattered them. From now on I'll live with the times.'

His voice retained its harshness, but Mary detected the disillusionment hidden in its depths. He'd thought her so good and fine, placing her on a pedestal – high on a pedestal where every woman longs to be. With a little sob she half turned away.

'I know you think you hate me now,' she whispered tremulously, 'but you won't always feel this way. It's because of how you feel that you won't make allowances – oh, I know I've done wrong,' she added as he would have spoken, 'but

I haven't committed a crime. The time will come when you'll admit that this attitude of yours is out of all proportion.'

'Are you actually trying to minimize the offence? What woman with any sense of honour would consent to take part in a scheme like that? – to interfere in the affairs of a man totally unknown to her?' She wondered if he were aware of his admission as he went on to say that she could have ruined two lives, had he still cared for Cleone. She felt the admission had come out by accident, but there was no doubt that his words impressed her deeply, bringing home to her the real seriousness of her action in falling in with his mother's plan. As he said, he could still have loved Cleone. What right had she, Mary, to take it upon herself to keep them apart? 'I knew from the first there was something odd in the relationship between you and Mother,' he went on as if the thought had just struck him. 'Her attitude towards you was always one of indebtedness.' His words brought back the remark he had made about Mary and his mother looking like conspirators ... and the odd glint in his eyes as he watched them. 'There's a lot I don't know about you, I'm thinking,' he went on, his dark eyes narrowed and searching. 'A lot that puzzles me. You said there were several reasons for your coming out here to Cyprus. One of them I've discovered,' he added harshly. 'Was another anything to do with the fact that you've no friends?'

She started visibly as her heart jerked in sudden fear. The hint of colour still remaining in her cheeks slowly receded, and an unsteady hand caught at the ends of her hair, twisting it with a nervous, convulsive movement. If he should ever find out about Vance. ... It would surely be the end.

'That – isn't kind of you,' she faltered, then added, 'I've made a few friends since coming here. . . .'

'Where no one knows you?' Her agitation was not lost on him, she realized, much to her dismay.

'You must say these things to hurt me, mustn't you, Adrian? You've never bothered to bring the subject up before.'

'It's puzzled me, nevertheless. But,' he added, his mouth curving bitterly, 'I couldn't imagine it being your fault, couldn't see you capable of anything which would cause people to shun you, but now—' He broke off, eyeing her with eyes that had unexpectedly darkened with pain, 'I don't know what sort of a woman I've married.'

Mary could find no answer to that, and she turned away, unbearably hurt both by what he had said to her, and by the unhappiness which he himself was obviously enduring.

After a while she realized she was alone and she ran out to the car, reaching it just as Adrian was drawing away. He stopped, but kept the engine ticking over.

'Don't bring her to stay with us, I beg of you.' With that inadvertent admission still dominating her thoughts she looked straight at him, her stare deliberate, and challenging. 'You've no real wish to see her again; if you do bring her it will be purely for revenge – to punish me.' There was a marked avoidance of her gaze as she said that, and dark colour slowly rose to dispel a little of the harshness of his face. 'You refuse to say whether or not she's coming at your invitation, but somehow I can't believe she is.' He now had no interest in her words; she sensed his impatience to be gone and placed her hands on top of the half open window in a desperate plea for attention. 'I don't want her, Adrian . . . I'm afraid. . . .'

'Of what?' An amused sneer touched his lips. 'Afraid she'll set out to ensnare me? Well, that'll make two of you, won't it?'

'I didn't— You've remarked yourself, many times, on the way Josie says silly things. Adrian, that's one thing you can't honestly accuse me of. I fell in love with you quite naturally; there was no need to – to—' A deep flush spread as Mary floundered, searching for words.

'Get to work on me?' her husband put in smoothly, and once again her indignation rose.

'I didn't,' she denied again. 'You don't know what you're saying. I never once tried to – to attract you—'

'On the contrary, you made several deliberate attempts to draw my attention to you — several that I can recall, but there were many more, I expect, that I didn't notice at the time.'

Mary gasped at that deliberate lie, but something in his glance caused her brow to furrow in concentration as she endeavoured to bring to mind any incident which would account for his accusation. And she remembered the occasion when she had tripped and fallen against him, involuntarily grasping his arm. Surely he knew that was genuine! Also, she had taken special pains to look attractive, and on the occasion when she knew they would be dancing she had used Josie's perfume on her hair. That had been deliberate, she had to own, but all women did such things. Surely he wasn't holding that against her? And yet he must be, for there was nothing else.

'If I did want you to notice me, it was only because I loved you and because I wanted you to love me.' It was the wrong time for such an admission. Her whole body sagged with helplessness and despair as she realized that in his present mood he was ready only to magnify anything which would show her in an unfavourable light.

'Will you take your hands off that window?' he said curtly. 'I want to move.'

Mary stepped back, tears starting to her eyes at the way he spoke to her.

'You w-won't let her see — see there's anything wrong between us?' she faltered. 'You wouldn't humiliate me to that extent?'

'I shall bring you down to the depths of humiliation,' he returned harshly, 'as you have brought me.' He let in the clutch; the car roared out across the concrete, following the lane through the orange trees. Mary watched until it disappeared, then slowly returned to the office.

But she couldn't work. She wondered if her husband would expect her to do so after telling her, baldly, that he was going to the airport to meet his former fiancée?

To bring her here; to ask his wife to prepare a room for

her . . . it wasn't fair—

Mary stiffened as anger surged up within her. For the first time since that terrible day she allowed the weight of guilt to fall aside. What right had he to bring another woman into *her* home? She couldn't prevent him from doing so, but if he thought she was going to see to the preparation of a room . . .!

For a fortnight she had humbled herself, desperately trying to regain his esteem, to earn his forgiveness. But he wouldn't bend. And now this cruel and calculated form of revenge. What did he think she was made of, to sit back meekly and take that? Covering the typewriter, she looked round and then, after closing all the windows, she went outside and got into the jeep. Adrian had told her to leave early and she was doing so, leaving very early, for there was still an hour to go before lunch. She had asked him not to let Cleone know of the trouble between them, and his reaction was to inform her of his intention of humiliating her. Very well, let him do so; Mary didn't care any more. Cleone would know of the rift as soon as she arrived – even if Adrian had not already told her – for Mary had no intention of being there to greet them. And if Adrian *had* decided not to tell Cleone of the trouble between him and his wife, then he would be the one to be humiliated. And it would do him good, Mary thought. It would perhaps give him a better understanding of the way she herself was feeling.

After collecting some provisions Mary drove out to the bungalow. The garden had become overgrown with weeds and after eating her snack lunch she began working on it. She put everything into her task, concentrating on it and not allowing herself time to dwell on what her husband was doing. A couple of hours was profitably spent on the borders, and Mary surveyed them with satisfaction, making a mental vow not to allow the weeds to run riot again. Either she would make time to come over herself, or she would get one of the men from the plantation to care for the garden as a spare time job.

Feeling hot and sticky, she had a cold shower and then walked over to the Sandersons' bungalow. It was her first visit since coming back to Cyprus and Joy bounded down the path to meet her. Her sister followed more slowly.

'Oh, Mary, have you come to tea?'

'Mary can't stay to tea,' said Pam, her manner more controlled, though she was clearly as excited as Joy at Mary's unexpected appearance. 'She has a husband to look after now.'

'I know she has a husband to look after, stupid. Have you got your wedding photographs, Mary?' and when Mary shook her head, 'I love looking at wedding photographs. Did you wear white? I'm going to wear white – if I get married, that is. Uncle Geoff says I'll never get married because I'm like a boy. And he won't get married either, because he wanted you.'

'He was only joking, you know that,' chided Pam, casting an anxious glance at Mary. 'Joy says awful things. Take no notice of her.'

'But Uncle Geoff did like you. I heard him telling Mummy.' Mary smiled faintly at that. There had been no mistaking the admiration Geoff had shown on that first meeting – or on subsequent occasions. And he had bemoaned the fact of her forthcoming marriage, saying he had arrived too late. Mary had only laughed, for Geoff was not the sort of person to be taken seriously.

The children had each taken one of Mary's hands as they all walked up the path to the house. Mary felt warm inside, and wanted, after the icy indifference extended to her by Adrian for the past two weeks.

Dorothy's welcome added to that feeling of warmth and Mary soon found herself actually laughing at times, as they sat on the verandah drinking iced orange and chatting. After a while Pamela and Joy went off, on to the beach, and Mary tentatively inquired about the business.

'Geoff decided to put his money in it,' Dorothy told her. 'He hadn't a lot, but we're managing. Kevin says we'll have turned the corner by the end of next year.' She gave a great sigh of relief as she picked up the jug to pour Mary another drink. 'We really thought we'd have to return to England. It would have been awful, for of course we sold everything. It takes years to re-settle yourself after an upheaval like that.'

'You wouldn't have liked to go back, in any case; you're so happy here. And it's wonderful for the children.'

'We love it.' She replaced the jug and, looking at Mary critically, 'How about you? Did you have a wonderful time? Tell me about the wedding and – everything.'

'Yes,' Mary murmured, an ache in her heart at the memory of those idyllic days at Menna's cottage, 'I – we had a wonderful time.' She went on to describe the cottage. Dorothy knew Wales and said she knew the area but couldn't believe there was a cottage there, right in the heart of the mountains.

'It sounds marvellous for a honeymoon,' she said, a twinkle in her eye. 'Imagine not seeing another living soul for a week!'

'Who never saw another living soul for a week—? Mary!' Geoff appeared from the path behind the trees. He was big and fair, with light blue eyes and a broad, rather boyish grin. 'So the bridge returns. How's married life?' He sat down and spoke again without giving her time to answer. 'Was it you who never saw a living soul for a week?'

'Yes.'

'They spent their honeymoon in a cottage in the Welsh mountains,' Dorothy put in.

'Good lord, what did you do with yourselves – apart from – er . . .?'

'Geoff!' Dorothy laughed and poured him a drink. 'You're embarrassing her.'

'Nonsense; no one's embarrassed these days. Wouldn't do for me, stuck away like that.'

'Not for a honeymoon?' Dorothy asked, the twinkle once more appearing.

'Not even for a honeymoon. I like a bit of life. What did

146

you do?' he inquired of Mary again.

'We tramped, mainly. There were wonderful walks.' She could not hide the blush that touched her cheeks at his earlier remark, and she didn't try. Geoff was now clearly amused at the idea of spending one's honeymoon alone in the mountains, and she thought of Adrian, and of how he had wanted to take her right away, to have her to himself. He'd wanted to give her a wonderful memory and her eyes suddenly moistened as she heard his tender words, 'It will be a week we'll remember for always. I intend to make it so.'

'Can't say you look all happiness,' said Geoff bluntly, eyeing her with a critical gaze, as Dorothy had done a few moments before. 'I always thought brides were all starry-eyes and glowing – at least for the first month,' he added with mock cynicism. 'What's up?'

'Nothing.' Mary shot him a startled glance. She hoped her misery wasn't so apparent that everyone would notice. 'I must go.'

'You can't stay for tea?' Dorothy asked, and Mary hesitated. Her friends would think it odd if she stayed, unless. . . .

'I'd love to, if I may. Adrian is out and I don't know quite when he'll be back.' This was true; she hoped Dorothy wouldn't ask for more details.

'Fine. I'll get it ready at once.' She turned to Geoff. 'Where's Kevin?'

'Said he won't be long. I'd have stayed with him, but he said it was only a bit of paper-work he had to do and I couldn't help him even if I stayed.' He looked curiously at Mary. His buoyant manner of a moment ago was fading, replaced by a seriousness which took her completely by surprise. He waited until Dorothy had gone, then said, quietly,

'Who's the woman, Mary?'

'W-woman?' Tremblingly she put down her glass; its contents spilled on to the table. 'I don't know what you're talking about?'

'Saw her in his car just now,' he said, with much expression. 'Just turning in to your drive, he was. Didn't attach much importance to it – surmised you had a visitor. Didn't even think anything when I saw you here – but when you said you'd stay for tea. . . . It doesn't make sense, Mary.' He shook his head. 'No, it doesn't make sense at all. You should be all eager to be with your husband, not leaving him to be entertained by another woman. Who is she?' he said again, picking up her glass and handing it to her. 'Take a drink, Mary, girl; you look ready to pass out.'

So they'd arrived. Was Adrian furious at the discovery of her absence? He'd question Anya, learned what time she'd arrived home, and realize she had left the office immediately after his own departure. He would also learn of her taking the food and would instantly know that her absence was intentional. Mechanically, she took the glass from Geoff and put it to her lips. All her defiance of a few hours ago was dissolved. Mary was frightened of what she had done. Geoff was waiting; there was a new and strange determination in his manner that convinced her he intended having an answer.

'She's just a friend – of Adrian's; they were once engaged—' The words slipped out before she could check them; it was too late to do anything about it now, and she went on, 'She came over today – for – for a holiday, I expect. It was natural for Adrian to meet her at the airport. . . .' The tears came. She couldn't control them and within seconds her whole body shook with sobs as the nervous strain of the past two weeks was released. Having taken the glass from her trembling fingers, Geoff sat with it in his hand for a moment, watching her. Then, putting it down, he rose and moved to the other side of the table.

'That's right, get it out of your system. Here, take my handkerchief; it's not all that clean, but the size is right.'

'Dorothy,' she cried. 'If she comes. . . .'

'She won't. I'm off to keep her occupied in the back for a while.' He dropped a hand on to her shoulder, a strangely comforting hand. 'No one'll know but me, Mary girl, so don't go adding to your worries.' His voice seemed suddenly gruff, as if he were trying to keep down some emotion. All Mary could do was raise her eyes in a glance of gratitude before the sobs began to shake her again. Ten minutes later he returned, eyeing her gravely as he stood by the table, watching her unconsciously tugging at the corners of the saturated handkerchief which now lay in her lap.

She looked up, her eyes dry, but swollen.

'Geoff . . . I think I must go home.'

'Like that? If this damned friend of your husband happens to be the bitchy type then she's going to have the hell of a gloat.'

'Do I look awful?'

'Terrible,' he returned bluntly. 'Didn't know you'd be in this sort of a mess. Can't keep it from Dorothy – I thought you could, but it isn't possible.'

'You could explain – tell her I had to rush off—' She shook her head and Geoff said what Mary herself was thinking.

'Just isn't done. Dorothy would wonder what had got into you – running off without saying a word – and after you'd accepted her invitation to tea. No, I can't do a thing like that.'

'But I must go home,' she said again.

He hesitated, then shrugged.

'I wouldn't, if I were in your position, but you know best. What are you going to tell Dorothy?'

'I'll just ask her to excuse me, and say I'll explain the next time I see her.'

Mary suspected that Geoff cast a warning glance at Dorothy, as she came out a moment or two later. Whether or not this was so, Dorothy tactfully refrained from questioning her friend and Mary managed to get away without much embarrassment at all, and without seeing either Kevin or the children.

'I'll walk with you,' offered Geoff when Mary told him about leaving the jeep at the bungalow.

It was half past five by the time they arrived there; Mary

had worked herself up almost into a panic and she now couldn't get home quickly enough. For she had convinced herself that Adrian, angry and hurt as he was, would be in a receptive mood, ready and eager to snatch at consolation. Would Cleone quickly discern this . . . and exploit the situation?

'I'll have to clear away the few dishes I used for my lunch,' she said as they entered the bungalow. 'Would you turn the jeep round for me, Geoff?'

'Of course.' Mary handed him the key, but he stood with it in his hand, twirling it round and eyeing the table.

'So you had your lunch here? Thought you were still at the office? Dorothy said you told her earlier that you were staying on after your marriage.'

'I am still working. I left the office before twelve. Adrian went then, so – so I came away too.'

'I see.' His eyes held perception. 'An act of defiance, eh? And now you're scared?'

'No, certainly not. Why should I be scared?' she turned her attention to the table, beginning to collect up the dishes. 'Adrian told me to leave early.' She straightened up, coming face to face with Geoff, who had moved over to the table.

'What are you scared of – what your husband will do to you? Or what the other woman will do to him?'

'Don't say "the other woman" like that, Geoff,' she returned with a flash of anger. 'We've only been married three weeks!'

'That's just it. Three weeks and you're sobbing fit to break your heart. Three weeks and your husband's having his old girl-friend over to stay. Doesn't make sense. How does she come to be here – did he invite her?'

'I don't know. I can't think he would invite her, somehow. Perhaps she decided to come over for a holiday. She knew Adrian was here and so it would be natural for her to contact him and – and perhaps ask him to put her up—' But Geoff was shaking his head and Mary stopped, fully aware that her explanation carried no weight at all.

'No, Mary; definitely not natural. I can't see any girl

trying to intrude into her ex-fiancée's life only three weeks after his marriage.'

'I've been thinking about that, and I'm wondering whether she knew he was married. We were married very quietly in the village church, and Cleone lives a long way off. Of course Adrian will have told her by now—' Mary shook her head in a little helpless gesture, and there was a long moment of indecision before she went on, 'She's been writing to him – before we were married – hoping for a reconciliation. And I think perhaps she's suddenly decided to come over and see Adrian, not knowing he's married.'

'That sounds more feasible than the holiday idea. How do you know she was writing to him?'

'I take the letters in at the office, at least, I did. Adrian won't let me touch them now. ...' She flushed, realizing what she'd done. Geoff was eyeing her from under raised brows. When Mary remained silent he said gently,

'You've gone too far now, Mary. Better tell Uncle Geoff the lot.' Mary shook her head and Geoff shrugged resignedly, turning his head to glance at the table again. 'You say your husband told you to leave early. Did he tell you to come over here and spend the afternoon at the bungalow?'

'Geoff, please. ...' She dodged past him and went in the kitchen, putting the dishes into a bowl in the sink. Geoff followed her.

'I've asked you a question, Mary; why do you evade an answer? You weren't supposed to be doing this, but something else altogether, weren't you?'

Her nerves becoming more and more taut as the delay continued, Mary swung round on him.

'If you must know,' she flashed, 'I should have gone home and prepared a room for his – for this friend of his. And I wasn't willing to do it!'

'And by heavens, I don't blame you!' He startled her by the sudden burst of anger; she saw his fist close almost savagely round the key of the car. 'What an order to give one's wife! What sort of a man have you married, I'd like to know?'

At that she calmed down. She wouldn't have Geoff misjudging her husband.

'He has an excuse for anything he does, Geoff,' she told him seriously. 'You don't understand – and I can't explain.'

For a moment there was silence before Mary began to run water into the sink. Eventually Geoff spoke, with a return of that gruffness in his voice.

'Don't want to be inquisitive – I'm not one for poking my nose into other people's business – bores me, usually. But you, Mary girl – you're needing to tell someone. I wanted to mention it as we came along just now, but thought you'd begin crying again. Better to cry here – where you can use my shoulder.' She did not speak and he added, on a note of gentle persuasion, 'You've let slip some of it, Mary. Can't do any harm to tell me the rest.

His gravity still surprised her; on all their previous meetings he had adopted an air of flippancy and Mary had concluded that he was not the sort of person ever to be taken seriously. Joy's words about his liking her flashed into her consciousness, acting as a soothing balm to her hurts. All at once she had an urge to confide, to release some of her pent-up misery and, if need be, make use of that proffered shoulder. Yet she said, in an effort to throw off the impulse,

'We don't know each other very well, Geoff.'

'All the more reason why you should find it easy to open up. Couldn't do it to an old friend – embarrassing.' Taking the cup from her he placed it on the draining board. Then he took her hand and led her unresistingly back to the sitting-room.

'The time,' she said feebly, still shrinking from the idea of doing anything which might even in the remotest way seem disloyal to her husband. 'I really should go.'

But Geoff had pushed her gently on to the couch, and seated himself beside her. And almost before she knew it

152

Mary was telling him everything, noting as she did so that a most odd expression had come into his eyes. This she didn't make any effort to fathom at present, but she was to recall it vividly at a later date.

'You can understand, can't you, just how he feels – so terribly hurt?' she ended, already beginning to regret this confidence, and not daring to contemplate Adrian's reaction should he ever come to learn of it. 'You won't tell anyone, Geoff? Never mention it to Kevin, will you?' Her tones were urgent; Geoff threw her a glance of reproach.

'What do you take me for, Mary?'

'I'm sorry.'

Geoff sat gazing into space for a while, his brow furrowed in a thoughtful frown.

'Yes, Mary,' he said at last, 'I can understand how he feels.' He looked at her. 'Frankly, I myself wouldn't be exactly in a mood of loving tenderness on hearing that sort of conversation between my mother and my wife. I think he acted with admirable restraint, in fact. Wonder he didn't do you a mischief – and you couldn't altogether have blamed him, Mary girl.'

'Even that would have been preferable to this silence,' she said, a catch in her voice. She was beginning to work herself up again, for Adrian would probably become even more furious as time went on and she still hadn't put in an appearance.

'I expect so; don't know what a woman's feelings are.' He seemed puzzled all at once. 'There must have been some other reason why you decided to come here, to take up this post? As you've just said, we haven't known each other long, but I do know that you're not the sort of girl to do anything rash like throwing up your job and selling up your home merely to abet this Mrs. Stanning in a scheme which you must have known to be wrong. What about your family – your friends?'

'I have no family or friends, Geoff,' she answered, avoiding his gaze. 'The reason I had no friends is another story.

But that in fact did have some bearing on my decision to accept the post of Adrian's secretary.'

'You were getting away from something?' he queried on a note of perception, and Mary nodded.

'That's something I won't talk about, Geoff, so please don't press me.'

Respecting her desire not to be questioned about this, Geoff once more sat musing, that odd expression again entering his eyes.

'Have you thought of writing to his mother and explaining? If she gave him the true picture that must surely help.'

'If he won't listen to me then he won't listen to her, either. Besides, what is the true picture? We did conspire to influence his life. I must admit I knew at the time that if he ever found out he'd consider our interference quite inexcusable.'

'And yet you consented? – ah, yes, for your own personal reasons, mainly.' He paused again in thought. 'There's another aspect to all this, Mary. If you hadn't allowed yourself to become involved in what he probably considers at present to be a grossly reprehensible act, you two would never have met. When he's finished licking his wounds he'll have time to reflect on this and be grateful.'

'No, Geoff,' Mary put in sadly. 'He's more likely to wish we'd never met.'

'Don't believe it—' Geoff shook his head emphatically. 'You're too sweet, Mary, too desirable for any man to regret having married you. Don't look startled, I'm not going to complicate matters by trying to become "the other man". I won't deny I'd have had a go at winning you had we met in time, but I never was one to eat my heart out for something beyond my reach. I like you though, and I'll be damned if I'll stand by and have you hurt like this. Must do something about it.'

'It's kind of you to bother,' she said wanly. 'But there isn't a thing anyone can do. I'll just have to wait, and hope that one day he'll be willing to forgive me.'

'I don't agree that no one can help,' Geoff argued with a firmness that brought her head up in surprise. 'Your husband heard that story in most unfortunate circumstances and, by what you've said, in a way that throws most of the blame on you. But only a very little of the blame actually does lie with you, from what I can gather.'

'Adrian will never see it that way, though,' she maintained in accents of despair. 'No, Geoff, I've to resign myself to having lost his esteem – and to hoping, as I said, that he might come eventually to overlook what I've done.' The time must come, she thought desperately, when he would want to live a reasonably happy life. He would then forgive her, and that was all she could hope for. Adrian would never forget. What she had done would remain in the background of his memory for always, standing in the way of that perfect marriage of which he had so confidently spoken. The recollection of those words, of the love in his voice and the tenderness of his touch as he spoke them, brought the tears springing again to Mary's eyes and Geoff automatically slipped a comforting arm about her shoulders.

'Mustn't cry again,' he said soothingly. 'Get your face all puffed up if you do.' A small silence and then, in some puzzlement, 'Still can't fathom this action of your husband's. Going a bit far, it seems to me, having this girl staying in the house.'

'I thought that at first, but I can see now why he's doing it. It's to punish me mainly, but I think it's also to let his mother know that he'll do just as he pleases.'

'Will his mother get to hear of it?'

'Adrian will take it for granted that I'll write and tell her.'

'And will you?'

'No; there doesn't seem any sense in upsetting her peace of mind.'

'Can't say I altogether agree with sparing her, not when she's to blame for this pickle you're in.'

'She's not entirely to blame, Geoff. In all fairness I

could never say that.' She turned as Geoff abruptly took away his arm and stood up, moving to the other side of the room.

'Your husband's here. A car's just coming up the drive.'

'Adrian? But how would he know I was here?'

'The obvious place to look – when you weren't at home.'

'Yes, of course.' Unsteadily she rose to her feet, trembling slightly. And as if to add to her trepidation there came the memory of that hint of jealousy in Adrian's manner that day in the office when she'd told him Geoff had seen her home from the Sandersons' the previous evening.

Not that he'd be jealous now, but she was very much afraid that he'd be furious at seeing Geoff with her here at the bungalow.

And he was. His dark eyes flashed his anger as he stood in the doorway, his glance moving from Mary to Geoff, and then to the crumpled cushions on the couch. He spoke to Geoff, his voice as sharp and cold as flint.

'Do you mind leaving?'

'I'll leave, certainly – but, Mr. Stanning, I think you should know—'

'Geoff!' The exclamation stemmed from the sudden terror that he was about to make some slip that would reveal her confidences. Adrian's eyes narrowed with an odd expression as they rested on Geoff, who spoke at once.

'Mary wasn't too good, just now at Dorothy's. Had a queer turn as you might say—'

'Queer turn?' Adrian glanced sharply at his wife. No mistaking his concern, she thought, staring up at him, her face pale, her eyes still bright, almost feverishly so.

'I'm all right now, Adrian, thank you,' she said quickly.

For a moment he seemed unsure, examining her face critically and only withdrawing his attention when Geoff spoke again.

'I don't think Mary is fit to drive the jeep. If you take her in the car I'll follow on with it; I can walk back.'

It was unfortunate that he still held the key, Mary thought, for the sight of it in Geoff's hand seemed to inflame her husband. Geoff's phrasing too was not exactly tactful; Adrian in his present mood would probably see it as a veiled but clearly intended order rather than genuine concern at the idea of Mary's driving the jeep in her present overwrought state of nerves.

'The jeep can stay where it is, thank you.' He held out his hand for the key, which Geoff instantly passed to him. 'And now, if you'll go. . . .'

The sun was already dropping as they came out of the drive; a translucent glow filtered through the palm fronds, and down on the beach the waves lapping the shore were tinted with gold. For Mary there had always been magic in the fleeting eastern twilight, and especially so during those brief days of her engagement, when she and Adrian would walk along the beach, hand in hand, planning their wedding and their future. Then Adrian would see her back to the bungalow, staying for supper and lingering afterwards. . . .

No magic in the evening now, with the shadow of her husband's anger all around her. Mary sat straight up in the car, staring ahead, wondering when that shadow would take more definite shape. She hadn't long to wait; they had scarcely left the drive when he said, harshly,

'Did you have to tell that fellow everything? I didn't know you were on such intimate terms.'

'Geoff? But I didn't. . . .' she began, then stopped, flushing guiltily.

'Don't lie! You've treated me to more than enough of that. I suppose you've told your other friends, too. Why didn't you get up and shout it from the roof-tops?'

Mary looked down, hiding her wounded expression.

'I haven't told anyone else. And I wouldn't have told Geoff—' She broke off on seeing his hands clench on the wheel at that admission. 'I was upset, and he sensed that something was wrong.'

'And offered you comfort, no doubt,' he rasped, taking a bend at a dangerous speed.

'He was sympathetic,' she owned, and a sneer blended with the harshness of his mouth.

'I'm sure your version of the story brought out all his manly instincts of chivalry.' Another bend was reached; Mary steeled herself for the last-minute application of the brakes.

'I didn't try to minimize my own guilt,' she returned gently, 'or make excuses.' A tear shone on her cheek, then rolled down on to her hands, clasped tightly in her lap. 'There's no excuse for what I did; I'm not disputing that fact.'

The humble admission seemed to have the effect of disarming him and for a while they drove on in silence, the cool, night-scented breeze wafting in through the open windows of the car. At last Adrian wanted to know why she hadn't done as he requested, and seen to the preparation of a room for Cleone. At that her humility of a few moments ago evaporated and her head came up in a gesture of defiance.

'It wasn't a fair request to make, Adrian. I'm not a servant.'

'I asked you to see that Anya did it.'

'You asked me to help Anya.' She paused. 'Where is Cleone? Did you give her a room?'

'Anya has now got one ready. I expect Cleone is unpacking.'

'How long is she staying?' Mary's voice remained calm, contrasting strongly with the movement of her fingers, now agitatedly twisting the ends of her hair.

'I have no idea.' All anger had left his voice, and there was a weariness about him, a listlessness almost. He seemed to have no interest in anything. Was he already regretting bringing Cleone into their house? Mary caught her breath as hope soared. If only he'd tell Cleone that she couldn't stay after all. ... Without this added complication they might reach some understanding, now that Adrian had broken that terrible barrier of silence.

'Adrian. ...' Mary waited a long while before going on

to ask her question. 'Did Cleone know that you were –
married?'

'No.' Adrian swung the car on to the rose-tinted concrete of the drive, then slowed down to proceed at snails'
pace, as if reluctant to bring the journey to an end.

'Does she know of the – the rift between us?' she queried
on a little note of breathlessness.

'Naturally; otherwise I wouldn't have invited her here,
would I?'

'You did that to punish me,' she reminded him, and noted
the slight inclination of his head, signifying his acknow-
ledgement of her accusation.

'And the punishment would hardly be effective if Cleone
were led to believe you're a happy, well-loved bride.'

A stab of pain struck at her heart at those words, for
she forgot all else but the fact that she had been a happy
and well-loved bride . . . for one precious week.

'You mean to continue treating me in this way – the way
you have for the past two weeks – while Cleone is here?'

He did not reply at once. The car slithered to a standstill and he applied the handbrake. Then he turned to look
at her, his face a mask of hate.

'I said I'd bring you to the depths of humiliation, and I
shall.'

'No matter how it affects your own position?' Mary's
voice was weak and cracked, because of the painful quickening of her heartbeats. 'Has it not occurred to you that she
could derive satisfaction from the – the apparent failure of
your marriage?'

'Apparent?' he queried harshly, and, without giving her
time to answer, 'I mean to repay you, Mary, no matter
what the cost to myself.'

She lifted a hand, in an involuntary movement, as if to
touch his sleeve, then instantly allowed it to drop on to her
lap again.

'Adrian, you've practically admitted you don't want
Cleone here, that you have no feelings for her now. Send
her away—'

'No feelings?' The harshness left his face and he spoke in softer tones. 'On the contrary, I found our reunion most pleasant, and I believe she did, too.'

'No, no!' she returned frantically. 'You're lying – I know you're lying!' Her heart throbbed even more painfully as this changing tone registered. Was he lying? – or had the meeting with Cleone revived some feeling of affection for her? 'I'm so confused—' She looked at him, her eyes bewildered, like those of a lost child. 'You've just admitted that you brought Cleone here merely to punish me, and now you say – you say. . . .' Her voice broke as the weight of tears pressed hard against the back of her eyes. 'What – what did you talk about – as you came along?' She hadn't meant to say that; the quiver in her voice would surely tell him of her fear.

'Old times.' He was enjoying her misery, exulting in his revenge. 'It's quite true that I allowed Cleone to come here merely in order to punish you, but I could still find my reunion with her pleasant, surely?'

Allowed . . .? That was the only word that stood out. Allowed. There was a world of difference between allow and invite. Had Adrian not invited Cleone, then? Mary debated for a while on whether to ask him once again how Cleone came to be in Cyprus, but soon admitted the futility of doing so. That word allowed had slipped out, and Mary was sure that if faced with a query about it Adrian would instantly resort to evasion.

CHAPTER ELEVEN

MARY dressed carefully, feeling that she needed the confidence of a well-groomed appearance in order to get successfully through the ordeal of dinner. Cleone was already in the sitting-room chatting to Adrian, and Mary stood for a moment by the door, watching them, for they had not heard her footsteps on the thick carpet which covered the hall and stairs.

Cleone's appearance came as a shock to her, for the older girl had somehow discarded that air of sophistication, of worldly elegance. Her pale gold hair was no longer plaited round her head; it had been cut short and curled slightly. It clustered round her face and fell on to her forehead in a subtle but deliberate state of windswept charm. It took years off her age. Of make-up there was hardly any sign and those long, perfectly-tapered nails were now quite short and unadorned. The dress Cleone wore was in a delicate shade of peach, modest and youthful with a high neckline and a bodice beautifully cut but too loose for figure-revealing. Mary wondered if this were the way Cleone had looked when she was in her teens, when she had been so attractive to Adrian, had won his love. As for Mary herself, she felt suddenly older than her years and wished she could return to her room and find something less sophisticated. But both Adrian and Cleone had turned, Adrian to throw her a flickering glance of disinterest, and Cleone to smile in a rather childish way, saying how glad she was to meet her again, declaring her surprise at the discovery of her marriage to Adrian.

'I couldn't believe it when he told me on the way here,' she said. 'I certainly wouldn't have come had I known, but you don't mind having me, do you, Mary? I can call you Mary, can't I?'

Mary came slowly into the room, murmuring words which

she could never afterwards recall. But she knew she hadn't extended a welcome to Cleone, and neither did she give her permission to call her Mary.

During dinner Cleone and Adrian talked a lot about old times, recalling incidents and occurrences, laughing when the occasion called for laughter. Mary sat listening, being neither anxious to join in the conversation nor encouraged to do so. In fact, she was being deliberately ignored by them both. Angry colour fused her cheeks once or twice, but firmly she calmed herself down again. She would remain completely aloof; neither should see just how greatly she suffered.

When dinner was over they all returned to the sitting-room and the conversation between Adrian and Cleone continued as before. Then Adrian rose, saying he had a telephone call to make. No sooner had he left the room than Cleone turned to Mary, her blue eyes half-veiled by her drooping lashes; but the triumph in their depths was apparent.

'You shouldn't have come here in the first place, should you, Mary?' Cleone's affected naïve and youthful manner of a moment ago was dropped; her words rasped gently, like the warning hiss of a cat. 'You heard me telling Adrian's mother that he still cared for me, yet you allowed yourself to be drawn into her stupid scheme, a scheme he was bound to discover – and he has discovered it, hasn't he, Mary?'

'Did Adrian tell you about that?' Mary raised her head sharply. She just couldn't believe her husband would go as far as that.

'He didn't need to. I already knew. Oh, Mrs. Stanning was clever, and I was deceived at first, but not for long. When I later considered your reaction to her announcement that you were coming out here as Adrian's secretary I knew you hadn't an inkling of what she was going to do. I told Adrian today all about it.'

'He didn't discuss it with you?' Mary held her breath. If he'd talked about it to Cleone she would never forgive him.

'His silence told me all I wanted to know. It was clear he'd found out. And what about the first letter I sent?' Cleone went on, watching Mary closely. 'I mentioned it to him and he didn't show the least surprise – didn't even say it might have got lost in the post – but just remained closed up like a clam. I take it you tampered with his mail ... and he found out about that, too.' Her lip drew back almost in a snarl and her eyes darkened with hate. 'What right had you to take it upon yourself to keep us apart? – you or his mother? And then to go to the extremes of marriage, knowing he still loved me. No wonder it's already broken up!'

'Our marriage hasn't broken up,' flashed Mary, her eyes sparkling. 'It's only a temporary storm – and we shall weather it, I'm sure of that.' Cleone was shaking her head and Mary went on, before she could speak, 'I don't know quite how you come to be here, but I do know that Adrian didn't invite you—' Would she discover the truth if she tried a ruse? There was nothing to be lost. Under a compulsion she couldn't resist Mary took advantage of her husband's recent slip. 'Adrian gave me to understand he hadn't invited you to come over and he also told me you didn't know of our marriage.' The merest pause followed before Mary continued, looking straight at Cleone, 'You came over on a sudden impulse, just to see how Adrian would react to seeing you again.' As Mary hoped, Cleone was taken unawares, assuming what had never occurred.

'He – he told you that!' Dark colour crept slowly under the pink transparency of Cleone's cheeks. 'He told you I'd phoned him from the airport here in Nicosia – telling him I'd just arrived?'

So that was it! Adrian had received that phone call only minutes before coming out to tell Mary to prepare a room. It had come right out of the blue, and Mary felt that under normal circumstances Adrian would, in his own words, have 'let Cleone go to the devil', and left her at the airport. But that phone call offered a handy tool of revenge at a time when, still smarting under his humiliation,

Adrian was filled with the burning desire to make his wife suffer. And, just as Mary had surmised, his move in bringing Cleone to his home was also an act of retaliation for the interference in his life. It was calculated to convince both his mother and his wife that he would do exactly as he pleased. What Cleone had just said proved that Adrian hadn't arranged for her to come, hadn't been corresponding with her. It also explained his evasiveness when asked why Cleone was here in Cyprus, and how long she was staying. Mary looked at the other girl, and her spirits soared.

'You asked if you could stay at his home and when he consented you must have been filled with elation. But of course you didn't know he was married.' Cleone was clearly put out; the tables appeared to have been turned and Mary wouldn't have been human if she'd stopped to consider the other girl's feelings. 'You had the situation all wrong. Adrian still loves me, but as you say he'd found out I'd – interfered in his life. You yourself have had experience of his anger, his bitterness, and so you can understand his desire to hurt me, to punish me for what I'd done. Your phone call presented a heaven-sent opportunity— I have to tell you, Cleone that, unflattering as it might be to you to discover it, Adrian has merely used you – used you as an instrument of revenge.'

For a moment or two it seemed that Cleone was defeated, and Mary allowed her spirits to rise even higher. Surely Cleone would now go, making some excuse to Adrian for her hasty departure. But as she watched the expression on Cleone's face Mary saw it change, saw a malevolent light enter her eyes and a sneer return to her lips.

'So he's used me, has he? You really believe that?' A harsh laugh broke; Mary shivered, recalling with frightening intensity the trepidation and sense of danger she had experienced on the night of her first meeting with Cleone. 'Why do you think he married you?'

'Because he loved me, I know he did.'

'Love?' Cleone laughed again, a laugh that grated on Mary's nerves and added to her fear. 'You little fool — it's you he's used! When I wrote he knew I was free. I told him we cared for each other still and he was afraid, afraid he'd fall again. And I think you know Adrian well enough to realize he'd despise himself for his weakness, and so in order to protect himself from me he married you.' She paused, letting that sink in, her eyes glinting with satisfaction as they regarded Mary's white face and trembling mouth. 'I wonder just when he asked you to marry him . . .? Would it be about five weeks ago? Would it be just after he received my letter — my second letter?' she added significantly.

In a flash Mary saw Adrian standing by his desk, with that harsh expression on his lips, saw him reading, and then crushing that letter — so savagely, displaying an intense emotion. Then, tossing it into the waste-paper basket, he had turned to her and asked her to marry him. . . . He had said it must be soon . . . and that was because of the fear of changing his mind, of succumbing to Cleone's charms should he meet her again. Pain dragged at Mary's throat. To think she'd been so conceited as to believe her own attraction was so great that his urgency stemmed from the need of her . . . the desire.

'It can't be true.' Mary scarcely heard what she said; her hands were clammy and the faint tinge of colour still remaining in her cheeks slowly disappeared.

'It's true enough, surely you can see that. As I've said, it is you he's used — to punish me, but,' Cleone added deliberately, 'he's sorry now, for he knows he's made a mistake. I sensed his regret even while he was telling me of his marriage, for there was nothing but bitterness in his voice. You have to face the fact that he still loves me; you've only to watch the way he looks at me, and to listen when he speaks.'

'No, he loves me. . . .' Even as the whispered words fell from her trembling lips Mary saw again that harshness leave his face, heard the softness in his voice when he'd said,

'. . . I found our reunion most pleasant. . . .'

'You'd try to convince yourself at this stage?' Cleone's white teeth showed in a triumphant smile as she watched Mary's stricken face. 'You were misguided enough to be led by Mrs. Stanning, to intrude where you shouldn't – and now the only sensible thing for you to do is get out; that's my advice, for no marriage can succeed without love.'

Vaguely Mary wondered if Cleone was speaking from experience; but other thoughts soon came crowding in, thoughts which filled her with anger – hatred even – against her husband.

The arrogance of him to stand in judgement, to torture by his silent condemnation, to mete out punishment . . . when he was equally blameworthy – more blameworthy, for he had callously used her, seized her as a means of escape from the fear of his own impending weakness. Whatever she herself had done, her motives were sincere; she had married him for love.

This anger and resentment burned fiercely long after she had gone to her room, burned stronger even than the heart-breaking knowledge that all Adrian's love and affection, all his talk of ideals and a perfect marriage, had been a very fine act. The thought of her own unstinted giving brought the tears springing to her eyes. Almost savagely she rubbed them with her knuckles and then went into the bathroom to bathe them. After a shower she slipped between the cool linen sheets, turning her face into the pillow. But obviously sleep was to be denied her and she got up again. Everyone had gone to bed and she did not bother about a dressing-gown as she went downstairs to fetch a book. When she returned Adrian was standing by the window, facing the room. Mary hesitated by the door, automatically pulling with one hand on a ribbon threaded through the low wide neckline of her nightdress. She felt the gentle ruching of the material, bringing it up above the graceful curve of her breast. There was a sardonic twist of her husband's lips at the action.

'Close the door, Mary.' The very softness of his voice

startled her. She felt the thudding increase of her heart-beats; her hand dropped from the ribbon, to flutter nervously, but she made no move to obey Adrian's command. 'I said close the door.'

She recalled his threat, spoken with loathing, that her acting could cost her dear. How would he treat her if he stayed? He mustn't stay – not in this frame of mind.

Her slender figure remained framed in the open doorway while his gaze burned into her. Her eyes were great pools of green with fear leaping from their depths, her hair a floating cloud of russet brown clothing her shoulders and contrasting delicately with the whiteness of her skin. Adrian's eyes flickered, then darkened with the smouldering embers of a primitive need. Slowly he came across the room towards her.

In panic Mary spoke, her words deliberately obtuse.

'What is it, Adrian? If it's something you want to discuss, then surely it can wait till the morning. I'm – I'm rather tired.' She kept her voice low, thinking of Cleone along the corridor, but she could not bring herself to close the door.

Again that sardonic twist to her husband's lips, and his eyes rested fleetingly on the book she held.

'Tired, are you? Well, that's unfortunate, because what I've come for won't wait until the morning.'

'Do you really think—' She spoke in tones of urgency, but the words came with difficulty, checked as they were by the tight little knot of fear in her throat. 'Do you really think I'll allow you to stay here after the way you've treated me?' She managed to bring a steadiness into her voice as she contrived to appear calm.

'You allow?' He stopped in the middle of the room to stare at her, the upward curve of an eyebrow revealing a hint of arrogant mirth. But his glance was devoid of humour. His eyes held all the bitterness, all the disillusionment of the past two weeks . . . and they still retained those darkly burning embers of primitive desire. 'I don't wait till my wife allows me to come to her. I come when it suits me.'

Mary's eyes suddenly blazed as she recalled her recent

enlightenment regarding the reason for his marrying her. He would *not* come when it suited him!

'You have the effrontery to come to me like this after the way you've treated me!' she flashed, clenching her fist. He seemed taken aback by the unexpected dropping of her air of guilt. Strangely this only served to increase her anger. 'It was your decision that we should keep to our own rooms – and now you can abide by it!' No sooner had the words left her lips than she regretted them. Adrian's nostrils quivered and a crimson flood of dark fury crept slowly and menacingly upwards under the tan of his face. The book slipped from Mary's fingers as, with a lightning movement, he reached her side, drawing her resisting body against him and at the same time closing the door with his foot.

'You're the one who's going to abide, my girl. You elected to marry me and by heaven, you'll follow the rules!' His pyjama coat was open. Pressing her fists against the hardness of his chest, Mary tried to free herself from his embrace, but his encircling arms were hawsers of steel, inflexible and cruel. 'I said you'd pay for your superb acting—' His mouth came down on hers with all the savagery of primitive uncontrol; she struggled, then lay passive till his hold relaxed. She remained within his arms, her lips trembling with pain and fear, her eyes bright with tears as the memory of his tenderness came flooding back to torture her. With a gesture of anguish she shook her head. Why waste time on thoughts like these? That tenderness had only been a sham. 'You said we couldn't go on as we have been doing, and I agreed. It's not natural. You're too desirable, Mary. You made yourself desirable by your acting – you let me know what you had to give.' He kissed her again, on her mouth and her throat, his lips less cruel, but merciless still. She remained passive, her white face upraised, when at last he held her away from him to regard her with the contempt she now knew so well. 'You've ceased your struggles? You're wise, my dear, for I intend to take – and enjoy – what I've paid for.'

The blood rushed back to Mary's cheeks.

'In that case,' she said in a suffocated voice, 'you'll take nothing. I earn my keep!' That must surely be the worst thing a wife could say to her husband, but Mary was past caring, and she uttered the words in a rush of anger and indignation, heedless of what his reprisal might be.

'You—!' The dark colour became intensified and his cheek throbbed as a nerve quivered, out of control. 'You earn your keep, do you? Well, we'll soon alter that. From now on you'll stay at home and concern yourself with your wifely chores . . . and your duties!'

Mary threw back her head defiantly, recalling his words about not knowing how he'd ever managed without her.

'And how are you to get along without a secretary?'

'I shan't need to get along without a secretary.'

'What – what do you mean. . . . ?' She knew what he meant; it was written on his face, plainly for her to see. She stared up at him unblinkingly, her eyes dazed and in-credulous.

'Cleone wanted the post, and she can have it. That will leave you free to look after your home, and your husband.'

He meant it, she knew, meant to have Cleone working at the office while she, Mary, stayed at home. Was it an-other act of revenge – another form of punishment? Or did he genuinely want Cleone working with him? Cleone had said he regretted the marriage, hinting that he was now willing to take her back. The only thing left for Mary to do, Cleone had said, was to get out. Was this what Adrian wanted? After his reunion with his ex-fiancée – which on his own admission he'd found pleasant – *had* he come to regret his impulsive marriage? Did he no longer wish for protection against Cleone's charms? Suddenly the answers to these questions were unimportant. The only thing that mattered was that Adrian must not stay here tonight. She would not let him make love to her in some unbridled way, merely for the satisfying of his desires. She wouldn't allow him to use her in that manner – not after what she'd learned from Cleone. With a return of spirit Mary was determined to have it out with him, to let him know she was no longer under any illusions as to the reason for his marrying her. He'd married her on impulse in order to protect himself from Cleone by acquiring the armour of marriage. Yes, she would tell him . . . and let *him* wear the shackles of guilt, for a change. He would leave her then, for surely he'd admit to being ashamed – ashamed of assuming that injured air of the accuser when his own conduct had been far more reprehensible than hers.

'Adrian,' she said, the light of determination in her eyes, 'you are not staying here tonight. I've—'

'And how do you propose to stop me?'

'Easily. You won't want to stay when I've finished talking—' His lips prevented further speech as they again pressed hard on hers.

'Talking?' he laughed, when his head was raised once more. 'What a waste of time. Come, Mary, you enjoyed it well enough on those other occasions – even though you didn't love me. But who cares about love these days? We'll take what we have—'

'I shan't let you talk like this! I'm trying to tell you that I've had enough of your contempt for what I did, enough of your fine airs of injured innocence. But you're not innocent – I might as well tell you, Adrian, that I know why you—'

'Don't stall!' His manner reverted to that of the dominant possessor. 'There's no escape for you, Mary, either tonight or any other night I choose to come, so you may as well abandon this delaying action. You'll find it far less embarrassing to surrender gracefully.' He picked her up, kissing her when she again made an effort to speak. With a little sob she resigned herself to what must assuredly be torture, but tomorrow he would listen. And tomorrow the marriage would end. She was returning to England on the first available plane, and in the meantime she would stay either at her friends' bungalow or, if they hadn't accommodation for her, at a hotel in Famagusta.

CHAPTER TWELVE

It was five days later that Adrian announced his intention of letting Cleone have the bungalow. He came to Mary in the kitchen and asked her for the key, standing there as if expecting her to produce it from her apron pocket. For a moment she could only stare, unable to believe he was still fired by that almost inhuman desire for revenge.

'I don't want her to have the bungalow.' Her eyes pleaded, but a shake of Adrian's head told her his mind was made up. 'This is the worst thing you've ever done to me,' she said, turning from him in order to hide the tears that threatened. To think of Cleone living in the bungalow where she, Mary, had been so happy – to have her handling all the things that she had used, know she was tending the garden ... it was more than Mary could bear. 'Must you do it, Adrian?'

'Would you prefer her to remain here?'

Something in the way he said that brought Mary round again with a jerk. Could it be that he himself wanted Cleone out of the house? She didn't realize she was trembling visibly as she said,

'You're making her leave because of me?'

'You?' The old expression of pitiless arrogance touched his fine features, but was gone instantly as Mary began to speak. Her face was pale, and her voice unsteady, but there was hope and courage in her heart.

'I intended leaving you – after that night – if you'd been unkind—'

'Leaving?' A frown crossed his brow. 'You married me for security; why should you leave?'

'I didn't marry you for security, but you'll never believe that. You overheard something and—'

'Are you suggesting I should doubt the evidence of my own ears?' he asked, and Mary glanced at him uncertainly.

171

Did she imagine things, or was there a tenseness about him? – a strange expectancy?

She shook her head, and there was no doubt in her mind that his eyes had dulled a shade.

'No, I'm not suggesting that. And I can't explain, so let's leave it.'

For a long moment he stared at her, as if in indecision, then with a slight shrug of his shoulders he asked her what she meant by saying she intended leaving if he'd shown unkindness to her.

'If you'd used me merely for your – your own convenience, then I would have left you.'

'Hadn't I the right to . . . use you for my own convenience, as you so indelicately put it?'

She avoided an answer. To tell him that in her opinion he had no right would mean telling him also that she knew why he had married her, and that his reason for marriage deprived him of the right. But Mary no longer wanted to stir up mud; she was fighting for their future, and that sort of retaliation would not help.

'You gave me to understand that you intended to be – well, ruthless.' Words became difficult, for Adrian regarded her with keen interest, awaiting what was to come. 'I believe you intended to hurt me, but you didn't. . . .' He stood close, and without thinking Mary put up a hand to touch his sleeve. He stirred slightly, but did not move away. 'I had no wish to leave you then, because it was exactly as on those other occasions, those times at the cottage.' She stared up at him wonderingly, vaguely aware that her statement wasn't quite literally true. He had treated her with all the care and gentleness of those other occasions, yes, but without the tender loving words he had whispered afterwards, far far into the night. 'It was your original intention to hurt me, but – but—' Her eyes held his in a question as a tiny stab of fear weakened the hope and courage in her heart. 'You found you couldn't be unkind, didn't you, Adrian? Deep inside you wanted to hurt me – but you couldn't.' In an agony of suspense she waited. Would he

172

deny it? Would he shatter all the hope that had entered into her that night? His tenderness had convinced her that he cared. And although she now knew his hasty marriage had sprung from the desire to protect himself from Cleone's charms, Mary felt sure that he had no real regrets about the marriage.

Her conviction had given her hope, a hope which had caused her to change her mind about leaving him, a hope which had stilled her desire for revenge, her wish to turn the tables on him and watch him squirm with guilt as she informed him that she knew exactly why he had married her.

Adrian stirred again and Mary dropped her hand from his arm. It was a moment of profound silence as they looked into one another's eyes, while Mary waited, fully aware of the opening she had provided for her husband to hurt her more cruelly than ever before. Her lips moved; an almost soundless plea was uttered.

'Don't deny it, Adrian. Please don't deny it.' And as she continued to hold his gaze she saw some of the bitterness leave his face.

'I won't deny it,' he said at last. 'You're quite right, Mary, I found I couldn't hurt you – not in that way.'

A stillness entered the room, and then a breeze floated in through the open window heralding the first of the autumn rains. Soon the island would be bright with flowers again, the autumn crocuses and hyacinths; the cyclamen that would clothe the high valleys and the squills and the sea-lilies which would bloom on the coast. Outside a bird sang in the juniper tree, sang for sheer joy as if to tell the world its heart was light.

Mary's heart was light, too, and full. She smiled through a sudden mist of tears, and a little while later when Adrian again asked her for the key to the bungalow she was able to say, though in a subdued and gentle tone,

'It is because of me that you want Cleone to leave, isn't it?' Before he could reply Mary turned. A pan of thick soup was about to boil over on the stove and, swiftly, in order to save herself the chore of cleaning up the mess that threatened, Mary picked up a tea towel and grabbed the two small handles of the pan, lifting it right off the stove.

But the towel had caught at one of the knobs; the pan was suddenly jerked back and Mary let out a scream as the boiling soup swished over the side of the pan, on to her arm.

'Mary – darling!' Adrian somehow managed to take the pan from her and with a wholly instinctive movement she seized a sponge, soaked it in cold water and dabbed it on her arm. 'No – you *don't* do that!' He was too late. The scalded part of the arm was stripped of skin; it was adhering to the sponge which Adrian took from her trembling fingers. 'Mary, my love—' He found a clean towel and wrapped it round her arm. The pain was excruciating; her face was contorted and she bit her lip till it bled in an effort to stifle her screams.

'Oh, Adrian. . . . Oh, help me. . . .'

She was at the doctor's in no time at all, but the short journey in the car seemed like the long road to eternity. The dressing gave her some ease, but the pain had travelled right up to her shoulder and the doctor warned her that severe pain could be expected for several days.

'Even then, you will have much suffering. These things take a long time to clear up.' She would have a scar, too, a bad scar that would fade in time; though it would be many years before it disappeared altogether.

'I blame myself, darling. All that was Anya's job.'

Darling. . . . Even the agony of her arm could not occupy her mind to the exclusion of that endearment.

'Anya wouldn't have been so careless,' she said, after a long moment of savouring that tender word. 'She wanted to do the cooking, but I told her to see to the bedrooms.'

'Anya is more used to these things. You should have let her do the cooking.' His voice held regret; he blamed himself for the accident, for despite his inability to hurt her that night he had kept firmly to his decision that she should stay at home. In fairness Mary owned to his having an excuse. It was simply a case of injured pride. No man wants to be told that he doesn't keep his wife, however true the statement might be. No, Adrian must not blame himself, and she told him so. The accident was purely the result of her own carelessness.

Immediately they arrived home Adrian told Mary to go to her room and lie down. When he came to her a few moments later carrying a glass of water and the box of tablets which the doctor had given him she was sitting on the bed, her face ashen. She felt abominably sick.

'You're all to pieces,' he observed, regarding her shrewdly. 'Nerves. Take these.' Mary swallowed the tablets, aware that the feeling of nausea was quickly passing. Adrian took off her shoes, gently pulled her to her feet while he turned down the cover, then he laid her on the bed, drawing the cover up over her. 'Those tablets are to make you sleep. Try to settle down now.' His eyes lingered on her bandaged arm, lying straight out on the cover. 'Is the pain very bad?'

'It is rather.' She tried to take her mind off the pain, but the bandages were tight and, Mary suspected, were also beginning to stick to the raw flesh. Nevertheless, she managed a smile, as she lay there. Looking up at him. His dark eyes returned her smile, but the tightness of his mouth remained. What had he on his mind to make him appear so grey and drawn? The accident, obviously, the accident that had brought from him that spontaneous endearment, drawing them a little closer together. But there was bitterness and pain in his eyes still and although Mary now felt confident that eventually they would be happy again she was not so optimistic as to believe the accident could by some magic process resolve all their difficulties. Moved though her husband was by her physical suffering, he was not yet ready to pardon her offences. But that odd light of expectancy in his eyes when she had denied marrying him for security convinced her that he was ready – or almost ready – to listen to any explanation she might wish to supply.

A tiredness enveloped her and she yawned. Some time, when she was feeling better, perhaps she could talk to him

. . . perhaps. . . .

He bent to smooth the bed cover and bring it higher up. She felt his warm clean breath on her face; her mouth trembled, inviting his kiss. His lips smiled then and he bent lower to take her offering.

'My Mary—' The words she had been aching to hear broke from him, escaping in a rush of emotion. 'My wife.' His lips touched hers again, so tenderly. 'Sleep now. I must go out, dear, but I'll be here when you wake.' He paused and a brooding darkness entered his eyes. 'You want that? You want me to be here when you wake?'

'More than anything, I want you.' Rather timidly she touched his sleeve. 'Are you going to the office?'

'Just for a short while. There are one or two matters requiring my attention.'

'You came home . . . especially for the key to the bungalow?'

'I came home for some papers I needed – those I was working on last evening. I forgot them this morning.'

'But the key,' she persisted, her mouth trembling. 'Must you let Cleone go to my – to the bungalow?'

'I'm taking her there tonight, after dinner. Now go to sleep, dear, and don't worry about a thing.'

But she did worry, causing a nervous tension to build up inside her. Why was he letting Cleone have the bungalow? she wondered fretfully. Why didn't he tell her to go? He had allowed her to come on a sudden vengeful impulse, and now he was sorry – he *must* be sorry— Unconsciously she moved her arm and almost cried out as the bandages dragged at her flesh. He didn't want Cleone, he *couldn't* want her. A querulous puckering of her brow brought an inquiring flicker to her husband's eyes, but she turned her face into the pillow. Why should he keep Cleone here? – he didn't need her— With a sharp intake of her breath Mary realized that the accident could result in Cleone's becoming firmly established as Adrian's secretary, for it would be a long while before she herself could use a type-writer. And besides . . . there was something else. . . .

Fear leapt into her eyes as she twisted her head to look up at Adrian's dark face above her, and every vestige of confidence deserted her. Supposing Cleone did stay on with Adrian – they'd be in the office together throughout the day, and it was an absolute certainty that Adrian would fall in love with her again. Yes, it just couldn't be otherwise. Without conscious volition she sat up, the sudden movement taking Adrian by surprise.

'I don't want Cleone to – to—' A flood of tears choked the words and within seconds she was sobbing in his arms.

'Mary, my sweetheart, don't cry. It's shock, darling, hush.' His hands were so strong, so warm and gentle, and so careful of her injured arm. She rested her head on his breast as the sobs continued to rack her body. She spoke hysterically; everything seemed to come out and yet she could never afterwards remember what she said. Vaguely it occurred to her that Adrian must be bewildered, not understanding a word that was so incoherently uttered. Yet he listened, his dark eyes kindling at times. After a while her tears ceased and she lifted her head to cast him a look of apology. He dried her eyes and her cheeks, automatically using the handkerchief to dab at the front of his shirt, where her face had been lying.

'I'm sorry,' she whispered huskily on observing his action.

'My Mary. . . .' He drew her to him again and held her close. 'You mustn't cry like that. Nothing is ever going to hurt you again.'

'Nothing?' She pulled herself away from him, raising her head. There was a desperate plea in the brightness of her eyes; she saw his expression change, and wondered at it. Was it something she had said in her hysterical fit of weeping that had brought that grimness to his face?

'Nothing,' he said firmly, and laid her back on the pillow. 'Now be a good girl and go to sleep.'

Adrian had gone to take Cleone to the bungalow when Geoff called after dinner that evening. Mary was in slacks and a white blouse which buttoned up the front, for the effort of putting on a dress had proved too much. Cleone's glance of disparagement at this attire left Mary unmoved, for there was clearly a serious rift in the relationship between her husband and his ex-fiancée. In any case, Mary's heart was now too light for anything, or anyone, to cast her down.

'I came as soon as we received your message. Dorothy intended coming, but Joy's a bit off colour, wants her mum. And Kevin's working.' Geoff took the chair offered and glanced with concern at Mary's arm, bandaged from the wrist to just above the elbow. 'How in heaven's name did you come to do a thing like that?'

She shrugged.

'Domestic accident; hundreds happen every day.' The pain had eased slightly, during her long sleep, but Mary knew the relief was only temporary. 'I was careless and I paid for it.'

'Damned painful, though; must be. Burns always are. Can't do much about them, either – just have to wait till the old cells get to work on the job of repair.' He glanced round. 'Nice place, Mary. You're a lucky girl.' His eyes became shrewd. 'Everything all right now?'

'We're happy, yes.' There was the merest hesitation between the first two words which Geoff caught on to instantly.

'Has he heard your version of the story yet?'

'No. But he's forgiven me, and that's all I want.'

'For now, yes, Mary girl, but the time'll come when you'd like him to know that there isn't really much to forgive.'

She nodded her agreement. She'd been thinking of that. Her relief at regaining his love was so great that she had tended to submerge the desire to regain his esteem as well.

'Some time I might try to tell him.'

'Some time? Why not now?' There was that odd light in Geoff's eyes which Mary had seen on a previous occasion. 'If you told him the tale exactly as you told it to me, he'd forget the whole unfortunate episode on the instant.'

'But I couldn't tell him in the way I told you,' and, when his brow lifted in a question, 'It's much more difficult with your husband – especially when there's his mother to shield.' An impatient click of his tongue was the only reply to that, and a moment later they both looked up as Anya came in with the coffee Mary had asked for. Geoff jumped up at once and brought over a small table, putting it close to Mary's chair.

'Better let me pour that,' he said when Anya had gone. 'Don't want a repetition with the other arm.' He poured her coffee and handed it to her. 'Your husband not in?'

'He's gone to the bungalow to – to take Cleone. She's having it for a few days.'

Geoff's head came up with a jerk.

'She still here? Still working at the office?'

'She's here until Thursday. But she doesn't work at the office any more – not since yesterday. Adrian told her she must go.' A happy smile touched Mary's lips at the recollection of the conversation she and Adrian had had after dinner while Cleone was upstairs attending to the last-minute details of her packing. 'He wouldn't let her stay here another night, even.'

'How's that? Seems rather silly to take her to the bungalow for a couple of days or so.' His blue eyes narrowed in a frown of perplexity. 'Something happened?'

Mary hesitated, but Geoff was waiting, his cup half raised to his lips, for her to explain.

'Adrian caught her in my bedroom. He heard a sound in there and knew it wasn't me because I was at the bungalow yesterday evening, gardening. As he went in she closed a drawer quickly, saying she'd been looking for a book she'd lent me.'

'In your room! Damned cheek. She should have waited for the book, or asked your husband to get it for her.'

'I hadn't borrowed a book. And Adrian knew that; he knew I'd never have anything of hers.'

'You hadn't—?' He stared uncomprehendingly. 'Then what *did* she want?'

'I've no idea, Geoff.' Mary shook her head in bewilderment. 'I've racked my brains and I can't think what she could have been looking for. There's nothing in that drawer except my private papers – birth certificate, national health card – you know, the things one usually has around – plus odds and ends, of course.'

'Private papers? You haven't missed anything?'

'Not that I know of. In any case, there just isn't anything she could want of mine.'

'Did she seem to have anything? Pinched anything, I mean?'

'Adrian said she had nothing in her hand. And as she hadn't taken anything he wasn't going to mention it to me. But I became so upset about him having her at the bungalow that he decided to tell me – just now, it was, when we were sitting after dinner. He was so angry at seeing her in my room, obviously searching my belongings, that he told her to leave at once. But there wasn't a seat on the plane today – there isn't one until Thursday, so Adrian let her have the bungalow. He wouldn't have her in the house another night. And he didn't have her at the office today. I thought she was there, but she'd gone off somewhere else, shopping probably.'

'Well, that seems to have sorted itself out. Why the devil he wanted her here in the first place beats me.'

'Adrian did tell me a little about that, too, but not much.' She paused, feeling she should not tell Geoff everything like this, but after some thought she decided it would not savour of disloyalty to her husband if she explained a little further. In any case, she did not see how she could now leave Geoff pondering over the matter of Cleone's appearance in Cyprus. 'Cleone herself had already enlightened me as to what happened.' Mary went on to say that Cleone, on not receiving replies to her letters, had decided to come to Cyprus and take Adrian by surprise, for, as she had told Mrs. Stanning, she really believed Adrian had remained single because of his love for her. He had only to see her and all would be forgiven. On arrival at the airport she rang Adrian and asked him to meet her. As Mary herself had surmised, his first reaction was to let Cleone return to England by the next available plane, but then came the idea of punishing Mary for the terrible hurt she had inflicted upon him. Adrian also admitted, without making excuses, that another reason he had consented to Cleone's coming to stay was in order to teach his mother – and Mary herself, she surmised, but Adrian didn't say so – to keep out of his affairs in future, to show her he was master of his own actions and would never tolerate interference. Mary did not mention that Adrian had married in haste in order to protect himself from Cleone. It wasn't necessary. Another reason why she refrained was that it showed her husband in a bad light, revealed a weakness in him which she herself had difficulty in accepting. He always appeared to have such strength of character that the fact of his marrying from a sense of fear came as a shock to Mary, and she felt it would be some considerable time before her disappointment at this weakness in her husband was erased completely from her mind.

'So she goes on Thursday,' Geoff said musingly when Mary had stopped talking. 'And you're all set for the happy ending. You deserve it, Mary girl.'

'Thanks, Geoff,' she smiled, and then, 'How about you? Is the business going all right now?'

His handsome face clouded, much to Mary's dismay.

'They're having the heck of a struggle. No money. Shouldn't tackle business without ample money. Too impulsive. Kevin always was.'

'But your money – I understood that had put them on the road to recovery?' A shadow crossed her brow. 'They said they'd have turned the corner by next year.'

'Probably; but I doubt it. My money did help, as you say, but that all went on new equipment – and now they're stuck with me as a drag on them.'

'Drag?' she echoed, puzzled. 'How can that be? You

work in the factory.'

'There isn't any work for another man, not yet. And they have to pay me something – I manage with as little as I can, but one has to have something. Also,' he added ruefully, 'a big fellow like me naturally has a big appetite.' His blue eyes were troubled and Mary now noticed the faintly drawn look that had appeared on his face. 'To tell you the truth, Mary, I'm thinking of getting out—'

'Oh, no! They need your money,' she cried in distress at the thought of her friends' business failing. 'Don't do that, Geoff, there must be some other way.'

'You misunderstand me. I'll leave my money in, but get a job elsewhere. I could still stay on with them, as a paying guest, and my contribution would help Dorothy with her household expenses. Good idea?'

'It's an excellent idea,' agreed Mary, her face clearing at once. 'What will you do?'

'Haven't thought much about it yet. Might get on a large plantation. I'd like that; could train for managing – or something of the sort.'

'You'd be good at that, I'm sure. What did you do before you came out to Cyprus?'

'Office work – anything. Dead end job. That's why I wrote to Kevin. Used to be called upon by everyone to fetch and carry.' A rueful grin spread and he sat thoughtfully silent for a space. 'Actually I had to stand in as private secretary once, for the managing director, for two months, it was. I liked it, though, liked it a lot.'

'Private secretary. . . .' Mary spoke to herself, her eyes flickering with an idea. 'Geoff, would you like to work for Adrian?'

'Your husband? Does he want workers?'

'He wants a secretary—' She broke off and laughed. 'I think I told you, he wanted a male secretary when I came.'

'By Jove, so you did!' He stopped suddenly, and his face fell. 'But you – aren't you going back? – when your arm's better?'

'It will be a long time before it's really right.' The merest pause and then, 'In any case, Adrian prefers me to stay at home.' Vaguely she was aware of thunder in the distance. A storm was obviously brewing. 'I don't want to push you off, Geoff, but if you don't start back now you're going to be soaked.'

'You're right.' He stood up. 'You'll speak to your husband, then?'

'As soon as he comes in, and then I'll ring – or perhaps he'll ring you himself.'

'I hope I'll be suitable. Like to settle here, have a bungalow and kids, maybe.'

'And a wife, of course.'

'And a wife, naturally.' He moved over as she rose from the chair. 'Arrived too late, didn't I, Mary girl?' But he laughed as she shook her head. 'No, I'd never flatter myself that you could ever be as starry-eyed as that over me.' His arm came about her shoulders in a brotherly gesture. 'You're damned sweet, Mary. If I get a girl like you I'll really believe in luck.' Mary turned to smile at him; he stooped to place a kiss on the tip of her nose.

'What the—!' Adrian strode into the room, his face blacker than any thunder-cloud outside. Geoff moved, dropping his arm to his side.

'Oh,' gasped Mary. 'You've been quick!' Frozen into immobility, she could only stand there staring, as her husband advanced towards her. It seemed as if he would grasp hold of her and she actually winced in anticipation of his touch on those bandages. But he jerked himself to a standstill, then turned to Geoff, his eyes smouldering, yet incredulous. Mary spoke wildly, her words born of the panic within her.

'Geoff wasn't holding me—' What a stupid thing to say. But that this should happen, just when the barrier between them was down. 'I mean, not in that sort of way.' That sounded even worse, and she was not surprised to see his smouldering gaze transferred to herself. But it was Geoff's expression that held her. The odd light she had seen in his eyes a few moments ago had reappeared; there was a slight hesitation and then he seemed to come to a firm decision.

'Mr. Stanning,' he said calmly, 'it's so easy to misinterpret both actions and words. If I may speak, try to explain. . . .'

Explain? Mary could almost have laughed at his optimism. Explain to Adrian while he was in a mood like this? Unwilling to stay and witness Geoff's discomfiture, she turned and went to her room.

She sat in the dark; the thunder was now overhead and rain lashed the windows. Lightning repeatedly lit the room with blue metallic sparks. What could they be talking about all this time? Why hadn't Adrian ordered Geoff from the house at once—? Quick footfalls reached her at last and nausea again swept over her. Her arm throbbed as if in sympathy with the wild beating of her heart. And then another sound registered, coming to her during a lull between the thunder claps. She blinked and puckered her brow, trying to concentrate. The jeep had been standing in the drive, alongside Adrian's car. Mary heard the starter, then the swish of heavy tyres along the flooded drive.

She blinked as Adrian snapped on the light, and said in a cracked little voice,

'You've lent Geoff the jeep – so he won't get wet?' Her heart still raced, but for a very different reason. 'He managed to explain, then?'

'Everything.' His face wore a greyish look of deep remorse, a look she didn't like to see.

'Everything?' With a flash of perception she understood that expression in Geoff's eyes. She also knew he had intended from the first to give Adrian her version of the story, should a suitable opportunity ever arise. 'He repeated what I'd told him?'

Adrian nodded. He stood close, looking down at her in silence for a moment; then he took her hand and brought her up against him.

'Yes, my darling, he repeated what you told him, and very different it sounded from what I overheard.'

'He must have explained it all very convincingly.'

'I was more than ready to listen,' he admitted, and went on to say that he had become convinced that she couldn't possibly be guilty of such despicable conduct. 'I learnt a good deal, too, when you wept so, after the accident.'

She looked up at him wonderingly.

'I didn't think you'd understand a word of it.'

'On the contrary, I learnt quite a lot. I knew even before Geoff talked that Mother was far more blameworthy than you—'

'Oh, no, Adrian, you mustn't think that—'

'I do think it; but have no fear, I can't be angry with her, for if it hadn't been for her interference you would never have come to me ... my Mary.' Despite the infinite tenderness of his tone she saw he was still filled with remorse and she put her arm around him in a gentle, tender way, and lifted her face for his kiss. But he did not kiss her; his eyes were dark and brooding and a shudder passed through him, as if he would shake off the weight of his guilt. 'What devil entered into me, to make me want to hurt you so? Why don't you shrink from me? I've been so terribly unjust.'

'But you didn't think you were being unjust,' she pointed out. 'I would have felt the same, had the positions been reversed.'

'Perhaps — but you would have been willing to listen to an explanation. That's what you meant when you said men were not so understanding as women, that they can be hard if things go wrong.'

'And you told me not to be afraid,' she reminded him, with a woman's subtle way of diversion while not exactly changing the subject. 'I'm not afraid, Adrian, because I know nothing can ever go wrong between us again – not any more.'

'Not any more,' he echoed fervently. And he stared down at her in a very odd way. 'I said earlier that nothing is ever going to hurt you again. I want you to remember that. Do you understand, Mary – fully understand?'

She shone up at him, her eyes clear and confident.
'Yes, I understand.'

Five days later her husband again strode in on Mary, and again his face was like thunder. She was seated by the fire in the sitting-room at The Wardens, an unopened book on her lap, her pensive gaze finding pictures in the glowing logs, but not actually seeing them. She started up, the book falling on to the hearth.

They stared at one another for a long moment, then Adrian spoke.

'Perhaps you will tell me,' he snapped, flinging his gloves across the room on to the couch, 'what sort of satisfaction a woman derives from making a martyr of herself!' And when, too mystified to reply, Mary continued to stare, 'Well? I'm interested!'

'I don't know what— Do you mean me? I haven't made a martyr of myself.'

'Not much, you haven't! Running back here – all sorry for yourself – instead of bringing your troubles to me. I told you nothing was ever going to hurt you again.' He unbuttoned his coat and took it off, tossing it over the back of a chair. 'How's that arm?' he said, momentarily changing the subject.

'The pain isn't too bad now, thank you, Adrian,' she returned politely, her legs gradually turning to jelly.

'Has a doctor seen it?'

'Yes.' This was ridiculous. What was he doing here? He should be hating her – after reading those newspaper cuttings which Cleone had stolen from her. They had been sent to Mary by Vance's mother, in a gesture of anger and spite, and Mary did not know she had kept them. Somehow, they had found their way into an envelope containing other papers. Cleone had taken the envelope thinking that it contained only the cuttings. She had returned the other papers to Mary, but said she was giving the cuttings to Adrian.

How did she come to have put them in that envelope?

Mary asked herself for the hundredth time. If only she hadn't kept them. . . .

'What did the doctor say?'

'It's doing as well as can be expected, thank you—'

'You can stop being so stiffly polite. I'm your husband!'

The heat from the fire became uncomfortable on the backs of her legs and Mary moved away, coming further into the room.

'I don't understand,' she whispered, trembling with sudden hope. 'Why have you come?'

A slight pause, with impatience filling the very air.

'I've just told you, I'm your husband. Why do you suppose I've come?'

Before Mary could reply Mrs. Stanning came into the room.

'Why, Adrian, when did you arrive? You should have let us know you were coming.' She smiled benignly at her daughter-in-law, at the same time looking very satisfied with herself.

'What do you mean, let you know? Seeing that you cabled me saying Mary was here I should imagine you knew damned well I was coming!'

'Oh . . . you promised.' Mary cast a reproachful glance at Mrs. Stanning, but received only a placid smile in return.

'No need to take on so, Adrian dear. Er – have you and Mary had your little talk? I didn't interrupt it, did I?'

'You're fully aware you've interrupted it,' was his ungracious retort. 'If you'll take yourself off we can proceed.'

'Adrian!' exclaimed Mary, shocked.

'Don't heed him, dear,' said Mrs. Stanning mildly, and actually giving her son an affectionate glance. 'Adrian is like that. Up, you know, on the instant. I used to be the same. Never let it trouble you, he'll improve with age.' She opened the door, then turned, smiling at them affectionately. 'Don't be too long, my dears, there's a meal in the oven – and I'm sure you could both do with it.'

'I'm still awaiting an answer to my question,' Adrian reminded Mary when the door had closed behind his mother. 'Why did you leave me without a word? – not giving me a clue as to where you'd gone?' A pause, and a faint smile accompanied by a shake of his head. 'Do women enjoy making martyrs of themselves?'

'I haven't,' she began, nervously twisting the ends of her hair between her fingers. 'I had to come away, because of Cleone. I thought you'd hate me when you learned about Vance.'

He ignored that, but at the mention of Cleone's name all his impatience dissolved and he reached for Mary's hand.

'She threatened you?' The words came out reluctantly and a frown of regret clouded his brow. 'Tell me about it, my Mary.'

My Mary. . . . Something tight caught at her throat, but the joy in her heart made words easy.

'It was on the day before she left. She told me she had the newspaper cuttings— She said, when I first met her, that she thought she'd read something about me and she mentioned it again one evening when you'd gone out somewhere. She said she'd remember, eventually.' Mary shuddered and went on, 'She gave the cuttings to you?' And when he nodded, 'They were in the drawer and she must have put them in her pocket when she heard you coming. She said that – that she hated us both—' Mary stopped. 'Must I, Adrian?'

'I'd like to know everything. I imagine you pleaded with her to return them to you?'

'I did. But she said you'd condemned her for the self-same thing, and she wasn't going to let me – get away with it.' Mary closed her eyes, re-living those terrible few minutes when she had begged Cleone to return the cuttings, or destroy them. 'I couldn't face you, thinking you'd hate me – why don't you hate me, Adrian – for what I did to Vance?'

'What did you do to Vance?' he mildly inquired, eyeing her with a calm untroubled gaze.

Mary caught her breath.

'You – you don't believe it?' she gasped.

'Not a word.'

So she'd run from him for nothing, that was what he meant when he said she'd made a martyr of herself, that she should have taken her troubles to him.

'But the newspapers—'

'Can be wrong, they often are.' He paused an instant. 'You can tell me about it some time, darling, if you wish, but not now. Go on, dear.'

'Well, as I was saying, I thought you'd hate me. You see, it wasn't as if you'd married me for love and I thought—' With a little gasp of horror she broke off. Never had she intended to tell Adrian that she knew of his weakness. She withdrew her hand from his and placed it tremblingly on her mouth, as she waited to see the guilty flood of colour rise under his tan. But all she saw was a stare of mystification before he said, rather brusquely,

'What the devil are you talking about? Where did you get the idea that I didn't marry you for love?'

'Did you marry me for love?' She felt the need to sit down, for her legs were refusing to support her. 'Didn't you marry me because you were afraid of – of falling in love with Cleone again, once you saw her?'

Silence ... except for the hissing of the logs as sap boiled and escaped.

'My God, Mary, is that the sort of man you think you've married!' His words flicked, and she averted her head, flushing under his accusing stare. 'You honestly believed I'd married you because I was afraid of Cleone?'

'You had that letter – the second one,' she added hurriedly. 'And immediately you'd read it you asked me to marry you.'

'What's that to do with it?' he demanded, his anger fading somewhat. 'Where does the letter come in? I intended asking you the previous evening – in fact, I'd begun to do so when your little friend – Joy, do you call her? – came along and interrupted me.'

'Was that what you were going to say?' she said breathlessly. 'You were going to ask me to marry you then?'

He reached for her hand again and drew her close to him.

'There have been so many misunderstandings, my Mary, but this about beats all. I love you, idiot. I must have loved you from that moment when you barged right into my office and demanded a job as my secretary!'

'Oh no, not then. You didn't like me at all— And I never demanded a job—'

His lips found hers, preventing further argument. It was a long while before he released her.

'I've got myself a male secretary now. Geoff's trial week has proved most satisfactory. He's going to be a good man to have around.'

'That night,' she murmured with a flash of memory. 'How scared I was when you caught Geoff with his arm around me. I thought you'd have killed me.'

'I shall never go quite that far, my love – but beware!' Mary laughed and nestled close and after a moment he said, 'Never leave me again, darling. There was no need this time, you know. I said nothing was ever going to hurt you again, said it very emphatically, but you didn't get the message.'

She looked up then, puzzled.

'You had an idea....?'

'Obviously you'd gone out to Cyprus to escape from something. You practically admitted it to me on one occasion. I couldn't have any idea what it was, of course, but I wanted you to know that if it ever came out I would listen to your version, would never condemn you. That was what I tried to convey, dearest, but, as I said, you didn't get the message. That was what made me cross – your not bringing your troubles to me. You will, darling, in future – always? That is what I'm here for, among other things.' He bent to kiss her and for a while no words were necessary. But then he murmured softly, amusement mingling with the tenderness in his voice, 'There wouldn't be anything else you would want to tell me?' He held her away, looking down at her, his eyes reflecting his amusement.

'No, nothing I can think of.'

A pause and then,

'I said I learned quite a lot when you wept that day. Geoff's coming was most opportune ... don't you agree?'

A soft flush rose and Mary whispered something about its being only an idea at present. And then she added, on a faintly anxious note,

'You do think it's a – a nice idea?'

'I think it's a wonderful idea—' He bent to kiss her quivering lips. 'A very wonderful idea ... my Mary.'

Harlequin Romances

TITLES STILL IN PRINT